TALL MAN RIDING

Matt Bray is summoned to his brother's ranch when his nephew, Tod, is kidnapped by outlaws. Because of his reputation as a gunman, Matt's family believes he is the only one who can help. Matt agrees, but the whole setup seems so bizarre that he wonders if his nephew arranged his own kidnapping . . .

But bloody deeds follow and Matt rides into a maze of deadly obstacles from which even a crack gunman may not escape alive.

TALL MAN RIDING

Ray Hogan

GUNSMOKE

This hardback edition 2002
by Chivers Press
by arrangement with
Golden West Literary Agency

ISBN 0 7540 8164 8

British Library Cataloguing in Publication Data available.

Printed and bound in Great Britain by
BOOKCRAFT, Midsomer Norton, Somerset

1

✷ ✷ ✷

"That's him," Linus Redfern said, looking toward the gate.

At the old man's terse words the half-dozen or so cowhands loafing expectantly in front of the bunkhouse came to immediate attention and threw their glances to the upper end of the yard. It was near sundown but the heat and glare of a hot summer day still lay upon the land.

"He's sure got the looks of a killer—"

It was Ferlin Shelldrake, one of the new and younger riders, who made the comment. Redfern shook his head, scrubbed at the sweaty, gray stubble on his chin. He had been around since the day the Brays started the ranch, some twenty years past, and held the dubious honor of being Rocking Chair's senior hand.

"You best keep something like that to yourself," he murmured reprovingly.

Ben Coy, leaning against the hitchrack, said, "He don't look much like the boss."

"Nope, I reckon he don't," Redfern agreed. "Don't favor the other two Brays neither. Sort of a kind all to hisself."

"Mighty tall one," Heck Stanley added. "Can see that even with him setting his saddle—and that's a big horse he's forking."

"Reason folks call him Six O'Clock—and was me

1

that named him that," Redfern said with a note of pride in his voice.

"That's a hell of a handle to tack on a man," Stanley commented, reaching for his cigarette makings. "It don't make no sense."

"Will—when you see him standing," the older man replied. "I got the idea when he was young-er—tall and narrow as a bean pole. Reminded me of the hands on a clock when they're straight up and down."

Ferlin Shelldrake's mouth split into a wide, un-derstanding smile. "I savvy! When it's six o'clock!"

"That's it," Linus said, and continued, thought-fully. "Don't seem like he's changed much. A mite heavier, maybe."

"And most likely plenty meaner," Ferlin said.

The old puncher frowned, shook his head. "Ain't figuring to tell you again, boy—you watch your lip. I don't want to hear nobody bad-mouth-ing him—nobody a'tall! Took a damn good man to just up and pull out, hand over half of this here ranch stock free the way he done. And what he turned into after he left the place happens to be his business."

"I ain't bad-mouthing him," Ferlin protested, "was only remarking on the looks of him. He don't exactly put a fellow in mind of a Sunday-school teacher."

Silence fell upon the men as they watched the rider draw nearer, pointing for the rack fronting the Bray ranch house. A small paint pony was al-ready picketed to the crossbar, the property of Karla Wagner, daughter of a neighboring rancher.

"What's he coming back now for?" Ben Coy wondered.

Redfern shrugged his thin shoulders. He had

the answer but had been told by John Bray to keep the reason for his younger brother's return quiet.

"Why'd he leave in the first place?" Heck Stanley asked when it became apparent Coy was to receive no reply.

"I heard it was over a woman," Frenchy Guitard volunteered. "Was him and the boss both wanting her and—"

"Now, hold on!" Redfern cut in sharply, and then brushed resignedly at the beads of moisture on his forehead. "Reckon you all might as well hear the straight of it right now. All this danged guessing don't do nothing but get stories started that ain't nowheres near the truth. I been here since the start, since Six O'Clock—his real name's Matt—and the rest of the Brays drove in and settled here, so I know what I'm talking about."

"Good," Coy said in a flat, abrupt way. "Always was one that liked to get the straight of things."

Redfern drew a plug of tobacco from his shirt pocket, bit off a chew, and stowed it away in a corner of his mouth. Squinting, he studied Matt Bray, now halfway the distance between the gate and the house. Then, folding his long arms across his chest, he leaned back against the wall of the structure that served as the crew's quarters.

"There was five of the Brays," he began. "They come here in the spring of fifty-five. John, he was the oldest. Was a widower and he had his boy with him."

"That'd be Tod," Coy said.

"Yep. Was two, maybe three years old. Next in line was Mark, and then come Luke. Matt's the youngest. I reckon he was around fourteen. They picked out this here place, started building. I was the first hired hand they put on, and right away they started turning this here valley into a mighty fine place. Them Brays all knew how to work, wasn't afraid of nothing and never backed off of doing anything.

"Matt was sort of my pet. He was always hanging around me, watching me doing something he didn't know how to do, helping me—and all the time growing straight up like a weed along a ditch bank."

Redfern paused, a slight frown pulling at his narrow, weathered features. Matt Bray had halted, was sitting ramrod stiff, a wide-brimmed, high-crowned hat pushed to the back of his head. He was staring off toward the low, grassy hills to the south of the ranch, as if remembering something.

"What's he looking at? Ain't nothing down there but the spring," Shelldrake wondered.

"Reckon it means something special to him," Linus replied, and passed off the question. He knew what was stirring Matt Bray's memory but it was a recollection that belonged to the gunfighter, and he would leave it that way.

"Like I was saying, things was going along fine, then the goddamned war come along. The Brays was all from Wisconsin and they had mighty strong feelings about the Union. Wound up with Matt and Luke and Mark riding off to join up, leaving John to run the ranch—not that it was taking much to keep it going; they had everything in plenty good shape."

"Expect you was the foreman about then—" Ferlin said.

"Yeh, reckon you could say that. Well, we didn't hear nothing from any of them, the mail being like it was during the fighting, and when it was all over only Matt come home."

"That what happened to the other Brays—they got themselves killed in the war?" Coy asked, frowning.

"Yep. Don't know much about it. John finally did get a letter from the army about the time it was all over, telling him they'd been killed, but he never talked none about it, just sort of bottled it up inside hisself and kept quiet.

"Fact was he'd taken hisself a new wife while the others was away, and he had his boy, Tod, growing up alongside him. I 'spect that kept him thinking about something else. Too, Mark and Luke had been gone four years and a fellow sort of forgets."

Coy nodded. "That the way he felt about Six O'Clock too?"

Redfern spat angrily. "Now, don't go getting no wrong ideas about John Bray! He was plenty glad to see Matt. They took up running the ranch together same as if there hadn't been no war. Only difference now was that Matt was half owner instead of only a quarter owner.

"He was a real fine-looking man when he come back. Growed up to six feet four, and while he was skinny as a rail, he sure had folks turning around for a second glance at him." Linus hesitated again. "Reckon that's what started the trouble."

"Was the boss's new wife," Heck Stanley supplied. "I heard that—"

"Maybe you ain't heard it right, but that was it. Lilah, her name was. She was a lot younger'n John, was about the same age as Matt, in fact, and besides being a real pretty little gal, she was a mighty fine woman. Don't think it was any fault of either her or Matt, but things just sort of happened between them—and the next I knew they was real serious about each other.

"Weren't nothing unnatural, you understand. Matt wasn't the kind to foul his own brother, and she sure wasn't one to do nothing wrong, neither. Me and Matt was still close after he come back, so I know what I'm saying. He used to do a lot of talking to me, confidential like, when we'd be off riding the range or seeing to the water holes and such.

"I couldn't help feeling right sorry for him. Lilah was the biggest thing in his life and he plain couldn't do nothing about it."

"The boss know what was going on?"

"Reckon he did but there wasn't anything he could accuse them of except feeling the way they did about each other—and you sure can't hog-tie a man or a woman's thinking.

"Time come, however, it got to working on Matt, so that he decided to move on. Told John he was handing over his half interest in the place and pulling out. And that's what he done—just up and left."

"How'd the boss take that?"

"Man never much knows how John Bray feels about anything. Just nodded when Matt told him, face as straight as a board, like it always is."

"You ever hear from Six O'Clock after that?" Shelldrake asked.

Linus was quiet for a time, faded old eyes still on Matt Bray now pulling up alongside the pinto at the hitchrack.

"Nope," he said finally, "nobody never did. Of course he probably didn't know about the accident when Lilah got herself killed and John lost the use of his legs and started spending his life in that wheelchair—leastwise I don't think he did, else he'd probably have come back and took over.

"I did hear about him a few times—trouble with the law, a shootout with some gunnie, him running with outlaws, things like that. Was always second- or third-hand and plenty old news."

"Appears he's sort of tamed down some from that," Coy said. "Heard he was working on a spread west of here when you sent for him."

Redfern wagged his head. "Things sure do get nosed around fast, for a fact! Only heard about him being there myself a few days ago! Sent word to him that John wanted to see him. Wasn't sure he'd come—but there he is."

"For sure," Ferlin Shelldrake murmured in an awed tone. "He's even tougher looking than I—"

"Never you mind," Redfern broke in sternly.

Matt Bray had drawn up to the rack. Still in the saddle, he considered the little paint standing hipshot in the lowering sunlight for a time, and then throwing a long leg over the back of the bay gelding he was riding, swung down.

He appeared to be even taller than the six foot four Linus Redfern had particularized, probably because of the peaked Texas-style hat he was wearing and the built-up heels of the boots, into which were tucked brown cord pants. A red bandanna was knotted loosely about his neck and his black leather vest was open over a gray shield shirt cuffed at his wrists.

Wrapping the gelding's lines about the crossbar, Bray wheeled slowly, threw his glance to the men at the bunkhouse, and nodded coldly. Dark-faced, with a full mustache and the faint shadow of a beard on his cheeks, he had flat, deep-set eyes that seemed to take in everything at once, at the same time assessing and making judgment.

There was a stillness to him, a lethal sort of quiet that established the idea of invulnerability, of utter independence and a total willingness to do whatever might be necessary to attain an end.

"I'm agreeing with the boy, here," Heck Stanley said in a low voice. "He's a hard-looking *hombre*."

"As soon shoot you as say howdy," Coy agreed.

Redfern shook his head slowly. The change that had overtaken Matt Bray was marked, and it filled him with a slight chill. He reckoned all the things that had been said and that he'd heard about him were true enough—but that wouldn't matter. Six O'Clock was still a Bray, and he wouldn't turn his back on his brother in this time of need.

"Expect I'd best be getting inside," the old puncher said, watching Matt move toward the house with long, deliberate strides. "John maybe'll be wanting something."

He started for the rear of the low-roofed structure, paused, looked back. "Now, I don't want to hear none of you bandying around what I told you about the Brays!" he warned.

"Don't you worry none," Shelldrake replied hastily. "I—we ain't about to do no talking about him!"

2

Matt Bray hesitated at the single, boot-scuffed step leading up onto the porch. How many times had he put his foot on it during the years he was growing up? How many times had he crossed the porch? Countless, no doubt—but that was the past, a century ago it seemed. But it all looked much the same—the boards in the floor warped a bit more, perhaps, and showing wear and the effects of the weather, as was the house itself.

And the hills, and the trees that grew around the spring where— Matt's thoughts halted. Why dredge up old and painful memories? It was pointless, caused the double-edged knife within him to twist and turn—more so now that Lilah was dead.

He'd heard about the accident one day while in deep south Texas doing a job. A rider who had worked for Rocking Chair passed through on his way to Mexico. John and Lilah had been coming back from town—Parsonville—he'd said. A violent thunderstorm had moved in suddenly as is the way of nature in that part of the country during the late summer months. Lightning had struck a pine tree close by the road, causing the team to bolt. A wheel of the buckboard struck a rock. The vehicle overturned, and when it was all over Lilah was dead and John crippled for life.

He had thought of returning to the ranch at that moment—the first time he'd felt the inclination since he'd pulled out. He decided against it. John could never forgive him for what had been between Lilah and him, and as for himself, the memory of her would be facing him from every corner and he didn't want that.

Besides, there was little he could do. John would have no problems running Rocking Chair. His son, Tod was grown by now, and chances were good he still had Linus Redfern and some of the other old hands around.

Best he continue the life he had chosen—one of drifting, hiring out to any man with the price to pay for his gun, and thereby keep the past pushed well into the background of his existence. By doing dangerous, often wild and foolish things, which fill the mind with tension and excitement, he had no time to dwell on thoughts of what might have been.

And so he had continued to wander aimlessly about the frontier, the name Six O'Clock that old Linus had pinned on him still riding his tall frame, along with a quickly earned reputation for superb efficiency when it came to using the pistol worn on his hip. But finally that had palled and he'd become weary of the long, lonely trails, and he turned to the work he'd learned before going off to fight a war—ranching.

He'd signed on in Mexico for a trail drive into Texas, and then later on to Dodge City where an unfortunate incident occurred. His reputation as a gunman being such, he was called out and was forced to use his weapon. It had been no fault of his—but it had cost him his job and taught him a lesson.

Thereafter he must stay clear of the big towns where he would be recognized, and thus avoid the ambitious gunslingers out to raise their standing among their kind, and the wet-eared kids seeking to prove themselves. To do that he'd find work as a cowhand on some back-country ranch where he was unknown—and could remain so.

The plan had succeeded. He had managed to be nothing more than Mathew Bray, with no talents other than knowing how to work cattle, and for almost a year he had enjoyed the simple, uneventful life. Then one day a letter had come.

Laboriously written, it was from Linus Redfern, who said that his brother John was in bad need of his immediate help; that crippled and chained to a wheelchair, he was unable to cope with a serious problem that faced him. Redfern didn't state what the problem was, only begged him to come at once—for the sake of their friendship if not for love of his brother.

Matt had mulled over the request for a few hours, not wanting to comply but finding it difficult to refuse old Linus, who had been like a father to him when he was growing up, and a close friend after he'd returned from the war.

In the end it was his regard for Linus that decided the question, and late that same day he drew his wages and headed north. Now he was back and the moment when he would be confronting John was at hand. He hoped only that they could get whatever the problem was handled quickly and he could be on his way.

Still, it was good to be back. The house with all its good memories, the hills, the grassy flats, the distant mountains like rugged, gray-blue shadows tumbling along the horizon—the sight of old

Linus standing down in front of the bunkhouse with some of the hired hands.

He could recall seeing him there innumerable times, just as he was now—old, lean, hawk-faced, and with his thin shoulders bent and slightly forward. None of the others looked familiar, and he wondered if Redfern was the only one left of the men he'd once known.

Stepping up onto the porch, Matt crossed to the door. Taking the knob in his hand, he again paused, his attention riveted by the ringing of a hammer on an anvil from the shed where a smithy was maintained. A man by the name of Josh had done the blacksmithing chores when he was a boy, had still been there when he rode in from the war. He wondered if Josh was still at it.

Twisting the knob, Matt pushed open the door and stepped into the hushed, heat-trapped front room that was designated the parlor. Nothing had changed—the pictures on the walls, the faded, flowered rug, the table with the family Bible in its exact center, the big rocking chair they had hauled all the way from Wisconsin.

It had been the only item of furniture they had been able to save from the fire that destroyed their home in Shullsburg, and was the source of the name they had given the ranch. It was in its customary corner, with the square footstool Mark had made from lumber left over from the house placed in front of it.

The touch of Lilah was there, too: the frilly lace curtains she'd made and hung over the windows, the antimacassars she had crocheted for the back of the leather settee to break its crude severity; the vase that daily in summer held fresh flowers from her garden was just where he had last seen it—perched on the darkly varnished top shelf of a whatnot.

"Who's that? Who's in there?"

He had no difficulty recognizing the voice that came from an adjoining room—the office, they had always called it. He could picture it now—bare floor, scarred roll-top desk, three or four hard-bottomed, straight-backed chairs, a calendar or two on the walls.

It was a bleak, graceless room, where John had spent much of his time working over his records, writing letters to cattle buyers, feed-supply companies, and other necessary business acquaintances, but to no one else, for John had no real friends. In fact, thinking back now, Matt realized none of them had had friends other than the men who worked for them and the merchants they dealt with in Parsonville, who could hardly be classified as such.

"Me—Matt," he replied, and slowly, reluctantly crossing the parlor, he ducked slightly as he passed through the doorway and stepped into the office.

3

✳ ✳ ✳

Bray halted just inside the room. The office had not changed but it was a different John he faced. Much older, thin to the point of emaciation, hollow eyes filled with bitterness, he considered Matt in sullen silence.

"Understand you wanted to see me," the tall man said quietly when it became apparent his brother intended to extend no greeting. "I'm here."

A girl was standing at the window to his left, regarding him narrowly. She was young—probably eighteen or so—huskily built, with brown hair, steady, unblinking dark eyes, and a firm, determined set to her lips.

"So I see," John murmured, stirring painfully in the wheelchair he occupied. He jerked a thumb at the girl. "This here's Karla Wagner. Her pa owns the ranch north of me. She and my boy'll be getting married pretty soon."

The girl nodded coolly, started to make a comment of some sort, broke off abruptly as the door leading to the kitchen opened and Linus Redfern appeared. The old puncher, ignoring both John Bray and Karla, grinned, stepped forward, and extended his hand to Matt.

"Sure mighty glad to see you, boy!"

Matt took Redfern's horny fingers into his own, smiled. It had been a long time since anyone had addressed him in that fashion.

"Good to see you, Linus. I was—"

"Hot in here," John Bray interrupted impatiently. "Open that damned front door, Linus, and let some air in here."

Redfern, eyes still on Matt, said, "Pleased you come," and moving past him into the parlor, swung back the thick panel that opened out onto the porch.

Matt waited until Linus had returned. Evidently John had converted Redfern into a nurse-maid since his accident, looked to him for all his needs.

"Rode up soon as I could get things set," he said, finising what he had begun to say. "What's this all about?"

"I'll do the talking," John cut in again. "If you got something to do, Linus, get at it."

"I ain't," Redfern said mildly, and leaned back against the wall near Matt.

The elder Bray favored the old cowhand with an angry glare, swung his attention to Matt. "You're looking just like I figured you would—a drifter, a damned gunfighter."

A hard-cornered smile pulled down Matt's lips. "You feel that way about me, why'd you send for me? As soon be somewheres else."

"Was Redfern's idea," John snapped. "I'd sure as hell be doing my own chores if I wasn't trapped in this goddamn chair!"

Matt shrugged. He should have expected it to be this way. "Well, far as I'm concerned," he drawled, "you can get yourself somebody else to do whatever it is. I'm not interested."

Karla Wagner stiffened. Her eyes flared. "You can at least hear him out!"

"Doubt if it would make much difference—"

"It should!"

Again Matt's wide shoulders stirred indifferently. Somewhere in the back of the house a clock ticked with hollow regularity, and off in the trees beyond the barn a dove mourned disconsolately.

"Expect there's a lot you don't know about my brother and me, girl," he said quietly. "Best you keep out of this."

"Keep out of it!" she echoed angrily. "I'll do nothing of the sort. It's as much my concern as anybody's."

"She and Tod are aiming to marry up," Linus explained. "Her pa, Karl Wagner—"

"John told me."

"Reason she's a mite worked up over what's happened."

It all had something to do with Tod, Matt reckoned, and John was finding it hard to call on him for help. He would be finding it equally difficult to give it, was wishing more and more that he had ignored Redfern's letter.

The silence hung in the stuffy, heat-laden room for a long minute, and then, finally, John Bray shifted his slight body and leaned forward.

"Needing a favor. Was why I let Redfern send for you."

"I know you're a bit shy on friends, but there ought to be a couple others around you could call on."

"Needing your kind. Didn't figure you'd come. Was a bit surprised to hear you was doing ranch work. Ain't much along your line, from what I been told."

Matt smiled. It galled John to ask a favor of him, so much so that he was delaying the request with idle comment.

"Haven't spent all my time robbing banks and sweating out the inside of a jail," he said dryly. "Can recollect doing a few days' honest work."

"But mostly what you been doing is farming out that gun you're wearing."

Matt drew up coldly. The expression on John's skull-like face changed to one of sly amusement.

"Tromped on your corns then, eh? Reckon you don't much like being tagged a gunslinger."

"Nothing to me."

"You ain't denying it?"

"Hell, no. Why should I? I've hired out my gun a few times. Man makes a living at whatever he's best at. It worrying you some?"

"Not one whit! I ain't proud of what you've done to the Bray name but we've managed to survive—and I expect we'll go right on living through it."

"Seems you've called on me for something—no matter what I am."

"One reason why, I can't do what's got to be done myself—otherwise I could live the rest of my life without ever seeing or hearing about you again!"

Matt gave that thought, wondered what had taken place between John and Lilah after he had pulled out. The bitterness in his brother was much deeper than he recalled, certainly greater than what he had expected after so long a time. It could have been the accident—the losing of Lilah, his own crippled condition. . . . The hardness within Matt Bray softened slightly. He should be more understanding toward John, he supposed; the man was to be pitied.

"You want to tell me why I'm here?"

The elder Bray brushed nervously at the sweat shining on his face, squirmed. "It's my boy, Tod— your nephew."

Matt folded his arms across his chest, stared off through the window. Tod would be about twenty by now, he guessed—and was apparently in some sort of trouble. He'd never had much use for John's son, considering him lazy, spoiled, and irresponsible, but that had been a few years ago and he'd overlooked it because of the boy's age. He'd probably changed.

"Was wondering where he was," he said for want of something better to say.

"He's gone—been kidnapped," John blurted out, his voice breaking.

Matt frowned, glanced at Linus Redfern. Both the dove and the anvil had silenced, and the room was filled with a deep hush. He brought his attention back to his brother.

"Kidnapped?"

"What I said! Got a letter telling me. They want twenty-five thousand dollars cash. If I don't hand it over to them they aim to kill him."

"You for certain it's on the level—that it's not some trick?"

"It ain't no trick! Was a note with the letter. It'd been written by Tod—and I know his writing. Said I'd best do what they said, else he was a goner. You think I'd be worrying and asking for help if I figured it wasn't straight?"

"No, I reckon not. . . . Where do I fit in?"

"Want you to deliver the money, and see that they turn Tod loose—alive—like they're promising they'll do."

4

* * *

A wry smile pulled at Matt Bray's stolid features. Asking him to help Tod was a twist; they had never been friends, although related, and Matt had avoided being around the boy whenever possible—a feeling shared at that time by all others on the ranch except his father. John, on the other hand, could never see his young son's faults and indulged him to the extreme. . . . But that, Matt reminded himself, had been years ago.

He glanced at Linus Redfern. The old puncher's lined visage was noncommittal. Karla Wagner still eyed him with suspicious intentness. He brought his attention back to John.

"What about the law? You call them in?"

"No—can't do that!" John Bray said hurriedly. "They warned me not to if I wanted to see Tod alive again. Said I was to keep the whole thing under my hat."

"Ain't even none of the hands knows about it yet," Linus added.

"Seems they'd wonder where he is—"

Linus scrubbed at his jaw. "Well, maybe, but he's gone off a few times before, stayed away maybe for a week or two. Expect they're guessing that's what he's doing now."

"Just like any boy with spirit—sowing his wild

oats," John said. "Ain't nothing wrong in him doing it."

Karla Wagner sniffed, plainly disapproving.
John threw an angry glance to her.

"You ruther he'd do it after you're married,
girl? That what you want—him out raising hell,
leaving you setting home by yourself—or you want
him to get it out of his blood now?"

From the sound of things, Tod Bray had
changed little, if any, Matt concluded.

"I don't think that's important," the girl said
icily. "Getting Tod back safely is what counts."

John considered her practical words quietly, all
the while studying her expressionless features. He
nodded.

"Yeh, you're right," he said heavily, and turned
to Matt. "Well, what about it? You ain't speaking
up like you was anxious to help."

"Long as you put it that way, I'm not," Matt
said coolly. "Fact is, I don't give a damn about
Tod, if you're wanting plain talk. He never was
nothing but a lazy, shiftless smart alec that caused
me no end of trouble—"

"You ain't known him since he grew out of a
boy," John broke in.

"No, reckon not."

"He's changed some. Anyway, he's my son—your
blood kin. I figure you owe me for all the time I
looked out for you after Ma and Pa died in the
fire. Was me that seen to it you had a shirt on
your back and something in your belly. Don't you
be forgetting that, Matt!"

"I'm not—and I never have. And I haven't said I
wouldn't do it—just want you to know how I feel
about it. Suit me fine if you'd get somebody else."

"Goddammit, don't think I didn't do some looking around before I let Redfern write that note to you! Goes against the grain something fierce to ask a favor of you, but I've got to have somebody I can depend on—trust."

"And somebody that can hold his own against them kidnappers," Linus said. "Would go myself, only I'd not stand a chance against the likes of them. Probably end up with them killing me and the boy both and then heading south for the border with the money. We figured you was the one that could handle them."

"Be dealing with your kind," John added, and then shook his head. "Hell, that ain't how I meant for it to come out. What I'm saying is, you've been around men like them, know how to deal with them."

The corners of Matt Bray's jaw had hardened as a stir of anger pushed through him. To his brother he was no better than the outlaws who had taken Tod, and he was being appealed to for help on that basis. An impulse to tell John to go to hell, to find somebody else, surged to the fore; let him make other arrangements—he could care less about Tod and what happened to him.

He glanced at the girl. She had scarcely taken her eyes off him since his arrival, and he wondered what her real thoughts on the situation were. Was she really interested in the safety of her future husband, or was she fearing the possibility of losing part and eventual ownership of the ranch? Somehow the latter seemed more suited to her attitude and actions, but she was a woman and he could be wrong about her. Seeing her standing there so resolute and alone brought a reminder of Lilah; she would have wanted him to help—regardless of how he felt about Tod.

Matt shook his head. "All right. Been enough said. Let's get down to business."

John Bray sighed. A slow grin parted Redfern's mouth, and Karla Wagner settled back contentedly.

"When do I take the money?"

"Been one of the bunch waiting for me to send it all week," John replied. "They set Saturday as the deadline. Letter said if somebody didn't show up by sundown that day, I'd find Tod hanging from a tree."

"This is Friday. Leaves only tomorrow," Linus said.

Matt swore softly. "Cutting it a mite close. If I hadn't got word from you—"

"They didn't give us much time to do anything," John said. "Aimed to have Redfern drive me down there in the buckboard, take my chances, if you didn't show up by noon tomorrow."

"Where do I go?"

"There's a fork in Redbank Creek—about ten miles below Buffalo Crossing—"

"I know where it is."

"Man'll be waiting there for you. After you give him the twenty-five thousand they'll turn Tod loose. I don't know where they're holding him. Ain't likely to be around there close."

"Not likely," Matt agreed. "Too risky. Somebody riding by might spot them."

"Now, money don't mean nothing to me where my boy's concerned. Going to put me in a hell of a bind, sure, and I can't afford to throw it away. Expect you to make damn sure Tod's all right and that they turn him loose before you hand it over to them."

"What I'll be doing," Matt said dryly. "You're forgetting your own words—that I'll be dealing with my kind."

John Bray swore raggedly. "Hell, Matt, I guess things can't ever be right betweeen us again. Nothing either one of us says comes out like it ought. I reckon she'll always be standing between us."

It was the first mention of Lilah that either of them had made. "Probably right," Matt said, and then looked directly at his older brother. "Like to think it would change someday."

John gave that a long moment's thought. "Maybe it can," he said, finally, "but it's a mighty deep cut. We get Tod back safe and sound, we can talk it over. I'll be doing some hard thinking meantime."

Matt was aware now of Linus Redfern's intent gaze, that Karla, frowning slightly, was again centering her attention on him.

"Don't know what there is to hash over," he said indifferently. "What's done's done, and there sure'n hell ain't no way we can back up time and change it. Far as I can see, it's a matter of forgetting, once and for all, and not talking."

"Forgetting!" John echoed. "That ain't nothing but a word. Are you able to stand there and tell me honest to God truthful to my face that you've forgot her?"

Matt made no reply for the moment, his eyes, half closed, reaching through the window of the stuffy office to the flats and rolling hills outside. Darkness was setting in and the shadows of the nearby trees were stretched full-length across the sun-seared ground.

"No—"

John nodded decisively. "Reckon you see what I mean then. Boils down to this—we'll have to learn to live with it, and I expect we can if we make up our minds to. Now, like I said, let's get Tod back here, then we can do some talking about your half of the ranch."

"Not my half anymore. Signed it over to you a long time ago."

"Know you did, but that's one thing we can sure back up on and change."

Matt gave that thought, shrugged after a bit. "Lot of water gone down the river since then," he said quietly, and added: "Get the money ready. I'll be heading out first thing in the morning."

Abruptly he turned then, his movements smooth and easy, and cutting back through the parlor, returned to the yard where he'd left his horse.

Linus Redfern, watching the tall man depart, bobbed his head. "Reckon I'd best see to him," he said, starting to follow.

"Expect he knows his way around here," John Bray said, somewhat stiffly. "He can eat here in the house with me, do his sleeping in his old room, if he wants."

"Expect that's how it'll be—he'll do what he wants," Linus said with a half smile, and continued on his way.

Karla crossed slowly to the window, her eyes thoughtful. After a moment she came about, faced John Bray.

"I don't like that man," she said in her firm way. "He scares me."

"Ain't no cause for you to be scared," Bray replied. "He's a hard case, all right, and I sure wouldn't want to be the man he held a grudge against, but we've got nothing to worry about."

Karla made no comment as she stood in quiet contemplation. Back in the cookhouse pans were rattling as preparations for the evening meal got under way.

"Did you mean what you said to him about coming here, taking up his half share of the ranch—or were you only saying that to get him to help us?" she asked after a long pause.

"Course I meant it! Ain't one to say something I don't mean."

"But you gave his part to Tod, said he was half owner of Rocking Chair and that he'd own it all when—"

"When I'm dead—"

The girl said nothing, let the words hang. Bray squirmed in his chair, swiped at the sweat clouding his eyes.

"Don't fret none about Tod. He'll still wind up half owner when I'm gone—figuring Matt comes back—and being half owner of a ranch like Rocking Chair ain't nothing to be sneezed at."

Karla shrugged, her round face downcast. "Hardly seems fair to Tod—"

"Reckon you mean to you—and Tod. You ain't fooling me none, girl. You got your mind set on owning this place, come hell or high water—and you'd tie up with the devil to get your hands on it!"

The girl's features darkened and protest leaped to her lips. Bray waved her to silence.

"Its all right. I ain't faulting you none. Fact is, I'm glad you're that way. Something Tod needs—a woman with an iron hand. But that don't give you the right to cut Matt out of his share if he wants it. I'm reminding you he was one of us that started this ranch—fought, scraped, scrambled, and worked like a goddamn mule right alone with Luke and Mark and me making it what it is today.

"And him being partners with you and Tod'll be a help. Let's don't have no dust blowing betwixt you and me when it comes to Tod. We both know damn well he ain't man enough to head up a ranch like this. There's more'n a hundred thousand acres of it, about half owned outright and the rest ours by right of possession, and we're running nigh onto two thousand head of cattle, even after that bunch the boys are pushing to Dodge City is figured.

"It takes a strong hand and a smart head to keep a place like this going—but that ain't all of it, not by a damn sight! Building up a ranch like Rocking Chair is only half of it—you've got to be man enough to hold on to it, too!

"That's one reason I'd sure like for Matt to move back—not because I've got any special feelings for him, but because, crippled up like I am, I can see things slipping away. I just ain't able to do what has to be done and there ain't nobody I can depend on. I need somebody to watch things—squatters, rustlers, them damn land grabbers—cattle buyers that'll rob a man blind if they get the chance, storekeepers and the like out to skin you all the time—"

"It'll be Tod that'll get skinned—and by him," Karla broke in calmly. "He hates Tod. Said as much. He'll manage somehow to freeze him—us—out."

John Bray wagged his head. "You're wrong

there, girl. Matt may be a lot of things, mostly bad, but he'd never do that."

"What makes you think so? I heard you say he'd ruined your life—"

"Meant it, too. It never was the same with me and my wife after they met."

"Then what makes you think he wouldn't stoop to cheating Tod out of his half of the ranch?"

"Something I just know, and this business with my wife don't change the fact that he's the hard-nosed, gunslinger kind that can hold onto this ranch for us—for you and Tod. Sort of like rattlesnakes. They're bad but they come in handy, too, keeping down the prairie-dog population.

"You get a mite older, you'll learn it's smart and practical sometimes to string along with somebody, whether you cotton to them or not, if they're the answer to a big problem you're up against."

Karla Wagner sighed, glanced out the window. It was full dark, and in the weeds along the foundation of the house, crickets were tuning up.

"I hope you're right," she said heavily. "I'm wondering about something else. What's to keep him from taking the money and riding on—forgetting all about Tod? He didn't get anything for his share of the ranch. He'll maybe decide this is a good way to collect."

"You don't know nothing about the Brays," John snapped, his voice hardening. "There ain't never been one that wasn't honest as the day is long, or a man of his word. Matt ain't no exception."

"He could have changed. The sort of life he's been leading—an outlaw, gunman, jailbird—"

"He changed the way he was living, not the kind of a man he was brought up to be."

"Could be.... Are you going to tell Tod when he gets back?"

"Sure. You think I wouldn't talk it over with him? I got a hunch he'll like the idea."

Karla smiled wanly, moving toward the door. "I hope so," she said again, and then: "Good night. I'll come tomorrow. I want to be here when Tod rides in."

5

✷ ✷ ✷

Despite his brother's wishes, Matt Bray chose to eat with the crew in the cookhouse and make his bed on one of the empty bunks in their quarters. This deprived him of the company of Linus, however, for the old puncher, because of his duties to the incapacitated John, was required to take his meals with the rancher in the main house and sleep in a room nearby so he would be readily available.

Matt ate alone at the end of the table, and bedded down somewhat apart from the other men. The crew left him strictly to himself, sensing, no doubt, something forbidding in his manner that closed them out.

Tired after the long day's ride, Matt crawled into his bunk shortly after supper was over. Sleep came quickly, but fitfully, and somewhere around midnight he rose, pulled on his clothing, and went outside.

The moon was bright, flooding the land with a pale, silver sheen, and the night was alive with its many mysterious sounds. He stood for a time at the corner of the bunkhouse staring out across the soft-edged hills and the shadowy flats while he smoked a slim cigarette.

Feeling restless because of the memories that came surging into his mind, he crossed the hard-

pack between the house and the secondary buildings, crawled through the split-rail fence he'd
helped erect to keep the stock from wandering
into the yard, and made his way to the spring.

His mind was crowded with thoughts of Lilah,
of John, the ranch, Tod—of what lay in the past
and what could be ahead for him. He was disturbed by his recollections of the girl, long buried
in the recesses of his mind.

He reckoned there was much in what John had
said—that she would always be there for both of
them, and that they could, if they tried, live with
it. But Matt was not entirely convinced, and having Tod around underfoot would not make it any
easier.

Tod had been a tribulation to Lilah, the source
of many heartaches. He had never accepted her as
his mother and John had done little to correct the
situation. There had been times when—

Matt, slumped on a log, listening to the soft
purling of the creek that flowed from the spring
while he wrestled with his thoughts, unconsciously
dropped a hand to the pistol on his hip as the
muted scrape of a boot heel reached him. He
should have no fears here on Rocking Chair, but
a man who has lived long with the dual com-
panions of danger and violence acquires the habit
of selfpreservation, a relentless master that dictates
automatic reaction to anything unknown and unexpected.

It was Linus Redfern. Bray settled back, the
tautness leaving his long frame and fading from
the flat planes of his face.

"Wasn't looking for company—"

The old cowhand grinned, gestured at the holstered weapon. "You sleep with that hog-leg strapped around your middle?"

"There's been times. What do you want?"

Linus moved forward, took a place on the log beside Matt. "Now, don't go getting your tail up. Just couldn't sleep. Seen you walking across the yard, and figured you might be of a mind to do some jawing. Knew this'd be where you'd head for, so I come."

Bray said nothing. Redfern dug out his plug of tobacco, bit off a chew, and sighed heavily.

"Sure is a right pretty night! That there big moon and all them stars make a man—"

"What's on your mind?" Matt cut in. "We've been friends too long for you to go beating around the bush before you talk up."

Redfern spat, raised a doubled leg, and lacing his fingers together, hooked them around his knee and leaned back.

"Yeh, you're right. Was wondering if you was aiming to take John's offer."

"He tell you to ask me that?"

The old man frowned, offended. "No, by jingo, he didn't! Maybe he's got me trotting around wiping his nose and such, but he ain't telling me what to say or what not to. Just wanting to know myself."

"Thinking on it, but not hard," Matt said, his tone softening. "Doubt if it'd work out."

"Why not? What happened was a long time ago."

Matt shrugged. "Years don't always wash out what's in a man's mind."

"Could, if he'd let them. Expect that's the big trouble—you plain don't want to forget anything. Was hoping you had when I wrote you that letter, but seeing you stop when you was riding in and take a long look at this here spring where you and her used to meet told me you was still carrying her in your head."

"Be nothing but trouble," Matt said, ignoring Redfern's observation, "not only with John but with Tod. You know how it was between the boy and me."

"Yeh, I know—and he ain't changed none for the better. He's worse, in fact. Never turns a hand around the place, always off somewheres hanging around some saloon, running with a bunch of no-accounts, and laying up with some doxy."

"When's he getting married to the Wagner girl?"

"She's ready now, and real anxious, but Tod ain't about to settle down yet—or anytime soon. He's got it too easy with John letting him get away with whatever he wants, anytime he pleases.

"Could be this kidnapping thing'll slow him down a mite, though. Heard John tell him the other day he wasn't getting no more money less'n he started in doing a little work around here and holding up his end. If he does, that'll change things some."

"What about the Wagner girl?"

"She's the best thing in the world that could happen to him. Ain't sure she'll be doing herself no favor, considering Tod, but tying Rocking Chair and her pa's ranch together'll make one hell of a spread someday."

"Kind of got the idea that's what she's thinking about. Struck me as being a bit on the grabby side."

"Way I see it, too, and I wouldn't be none surprised if John ain't figuring the same. She'd put a little iron in the boy's backbone—which he sure needs."

Matt Bray flipped the cold cigarette butt that had been hanging from a corner of his mouth off into the grass, drew out his sack of tobacco and papers, and began to roll another. Off in the night an owl hooted softly, and in the distant, higher hills a wolf howled into the pale glow.

"Probably the reason John wants me back—so's I can look after Tod and her."

"More'n likely," Redfern admitted frankly. "He ain't in no shape to do nothing—and we got squatters and rustlers nibbling at us from all sides. Unless somebody big enough and strong enough takes hold, Rocking Chair's going to go to hell in a few years."

Linus paused, splattered a nearby rock with brown juice. "It be so bad, you coming back and taking over? Could make a fine life for yourself—and it seems you ought to be thinking some now about settling down."

"Doubt if there's not a man alive who hasn't, and I have, I reckon. Quit the trails and the towns, been doing ranch work for some time now."

"For thirty dollars a month and found! Hell, Matt, you'd be a rich man here!"

"A rich man with a lot of worries and plenty of problems. Even if I could manage to get along with John, there'd still be Tod—and that cold-steel butterfly he'll be married to."

"You could keep them out of your way—send them off to buy cattle or feed, something like that."

"Hell, Linus, you know I couldn't trust him to do anything—and the day might come when I'd have to kill him."

Redfern allowed his leg to fall, drew up slowly. "You mean that, boy? You truly do?"

"I've got no use for Tod, and from what you tell me he's worse now than when I last saw him. Wouldn't want it to ever come down to gunplay, but a man can get forced into a situation where it's the only answer."

Linus shifted wearily. "Never figured to hear you say something like that," he muttered. "Hell, he's your nephew—blood kin!"

"That's no reason for letting him get by with what I wouldn't take from a stranger. He'd treat me the same way—and you know it—so why should I make any allowances for him because he's blood kin?"

Redfern was quiet for a long minute, and then he stirred again. "Things sure has changed with how folks look at things—with you a'plenty. I recollect when you and your brothers first come here, standing shoulder to shoulder—"

"That was a lot of years back—and things've changed, for sure. The way it was then and how it is now are two different matters."

"Maybe. You for certain it ain't Lilah that's done the changing?"

Bray gave that honest thought. "Could be a part of it—but it's not all. Mostly, it was that I had to find a new way to live, and I expect my values sort of changed."

"And you can't find no room in the man you are today for the Tods—that it?"

"Only if I'm pushed, and that's what would

happen here. I've never killed a man unless I was crowded into doing it."

"Then I take it that's your answer. Long as he's around you ain't interested in coming back—"

"About the size of it, Linus."

"Even if we was to work something out so's Tod wouldn't be around?"

"Might do a little thinking about it then."

"Well, I reckon I know where you stand," Redfern said, drawing himself erect. "Was hoping you could see your way clear to do it. Place needs you real bad. All the hard work you and your brothers done is going for nothing, I'm afraid, if you don't take hold. Could turn yourself into a mighty big man instead of—"

"I've got no regrets for what I've been—"

"Didn't say you did, just that it's awful hard to savvy why you ain't willing to take over what's rightfully yours. Best you know that paying that ransom money's going to knock a big hole in John's poke, and unless he can get some help running the place it could ruin him."

The wolf was being answered by a coyote, well off at a safe distance from his fiercer kind. The discordant yapping seemed to hang in the stilled, silver-shot air.

"Might work it out if Tod wasn't going to be underfoot."

Linus turned to start back for the house. He paused. "Just so's I've got my thinking straight—you're saying you might do it if John got rid of Tod—maybe sent him off to live somewheres else—that it?"

Matt nodded slowly. "Would make a difference. Other things to consider, too."

The old puncher's shoulders lifted, then fell.

"Only wanted to be sure," he murmured, and moved on. "Good night."

" 'Night," Matt Bray replied, and tossing his cold cigarette aside, began to roll another.

6

✷ ✷ ✷

It was early morning when Matt Bray rode out of the yard and pointed the bay south for the fork in Redbank Creek.

He had not talked with his brother before departing, had relied on Linus Redfern to bring him the ransom money while he was getting his horse ready—twenty-five thousand dollars in currency, distributed in a pair of saddlebags. When all was set, he mounted up, and with only a nod to the old cowhand, moved off.

He was giving the talk he'd had with Redfern no thought, his mind now centered wholly on the job that lay ahead of him. It would be tricky, he knew from experience. The outlaws wouldn't like leaving anyone alive who could later identify them—and that would include not only Tod but himself as well. He'd need to handle the transaction skillfully.

Tod no doubt was still alive. The kidnappers—number unknown, but probably several—would keep the boy alive in order to guarantee delivery of the money. Once that was accomplished, and they held all the high cards, it would become a different matter. But it was impossible to lay any hard and fast plan until he became aware of what he was up against; he would simply have to face whatever problem there was at that moment and overcome it.

Bray rode steadily, keeping the bay to a comfortable trot while he took in all the old familiar landmarks and sights of the country he'd once known so well. Little had changed over the years; the trees were larger, seemed less plentiful, and the grass, graying now in the late-summer heat, did not extend so far in all directions as he had recalled. And there was less color, fewer patches of bright flowers and vines.

He guessed there was truth in the old saw that a man could never really go home again, because it was never as he remembered it. Things tend to build up in his mind, become exaggerated, and conspire with time and absence to create a memory-picture that forever proves false; thus it is not the same. A man was foolish, he decided, to expect his world to stand still for him while he was away.

Redbank Creek was just ahead. He had taken a direct, cross-country route, ignoring the road that would have taken him by Buffalo Crossing, the settlement that hunched along the stream's deep cut, clay banks. It had been years since he'd last been there and he wondered if it had grown to any extent.

The town was not on any of the main roads, and existed largely because of the patronage of trail hands, gamblers, outlaws, and the like, there being only a few ranchers and homesteaders in the vicinity. It had never enjoyed Rocking Chair's business or that of other cattlemen living west of Slaughter Mountain. They found Parsonville, a quiet, staid little village, more to their liking.

The forks would be no more than five miles on

downstream. Matt halted at the edge of the creek, running shallow bank to bank with sluggish, silted water, and gave that thought. The area would be where the brush grew tall and thick—a spot well chosen by the outlaws.

Roweling the bay gelding lightly, he rode on. He'd move in easy, quietly, not leave himself open to a trap of some sort. It would please the outlaws mightily to bushwhack him, take the money, and be on their way without ever having been seen— except by Tod Bray.

They'd kill John's boy if that was the way it worked out—and he had to prevent that. A hard smile pulled at Bray's mouth. Here he was think- ing of how to keep Tod alive, when only the night before he had rocked his old friend Linus Red- fern back on his heels by saying he might one day be forced to kill the boy should he decide to re- claim his interest in Rocking Chair.

But there was a difference. This was a matter of saving Tod, regardless of personal feelings, for the sake of his brother John. He felt indebted to John, and it had nothing to do with the low opin- ion he had of his nephew.

Abruptly Matt drew to a halt. The faint smell of smoke was coming to him from downstream. He was near the point where the creek split, one channel flowing on southward, the other meander- ing leisurely off to the east where it served a scat- ter of homesteaders struggling to eke a livelihood from the reluctant soil in what people called Skull Valley.

It had to be the outlaw camp—Bray knew he was that close. Either they were having a late breakfast or were keeping a pot of coffee warming over a fire. Matt glanced about, swung the gelding hard right onto a fairly steep slope, and guided him through the rocks and brush until he judged he was opposite the fork. There, coming off the saddle, he tied the big horse to a clump of oak and headed downgrade for the stream. Coming to the last of the rank growth, he halted, peered through the thin screen of leaves and branches.

There was only one man in sight—a slumped figure, back to a large rock, dozing in the warm sunlight. A blackened coffee pot grumbled and steamed on a low fire nearby.

There had to be others. Matt, crouching lower, studied the area carefully. The camp had been pitched in the center island lying in the hollow created by the fork, where the banks sloped down to ground level. No attempt had been made to conceal its location—which could attest to the fact the outlaws believed they were holding the whip and need fear nothing insofar as John Bray was concerned.

Where were the others?

Understanding came to Matt in that next moment. That was the key to the outlaws' plan. Only one member of the gang was present at the point where the money was to be delivered. The rest, with Tod, were waiting elsewhere, safe and out of sight until the ransom was handed over. Like as not they had taken turns at manning the camp, knowing that John Bray would get the money to them sometime within the specified period. It was a good, thoughtfully conceived scheme—one that could work to their advantage several ways.

Wheeling, Matt retraced his steps to where the bay was tethered, and jerking the lines free, swung onto the saddle. Then, sitting tall and straight, he rode down into the camp.

He was almost upon the sleeping outlaw, features hidden by the hat tipped forward over his eyes, before the man realized it. He came suddenly awake, springing to his feet. His hand dropped to the gun at his hip, then slowly fell away as he stared up at Bray.

"You'" he blurted.

Matt nodded coldly. The outlaw was Jake Cooney from down south Texas way.

"Little out of your territory, ain't you, Jake?"

Cooney, over his surprise, shrugged. Slowly and carefully he raised his arms and folded them across his chest.

"Might say the same for you—"

"You'd be wrong. Grew up around here."

A frown twisted Cooney's bearded features, and then realization widened his red-rimmed eyes. "Say, you ain't no kin to—"

"Boy you're holding for ransom's my nephew. I'm here to get him."

Jake Cooney swore, wagged his head in wonderment. "I sure never hooked you two up together. Same name, but I reckon I didn't do no thinking on it—and there for certain ain't no family resemblance!"

"Where is he?" Matt said, voice still even. He didn't like Cooney—not because he was an outlaw, for there were many of like calling whom he respected as men, but because Jake was a sneak, a conniver who would shoot his best friend in the back for a silver dollar.

Jake turned his head, spat into the murky water, and grinned. "Right where we want him. You got the money?"

Matt patted the leather pouches hanging from

the horn of his saddle. "Twenty-five thousand in paper, just like the letter said."

Cooney took a step forward, extended his arm. "Hand it over."

Bray laughed. "You think I'm some kind of a damn fool, Jake? Get the boy. I'll turn the cash over to you at the same time you hand him over to me."

The outlaw frowned, scratched at the stubble on his jaw. A short distance beyond him in the stream a fish rose suddenly, snapped up an insect, and disappeared in a flash of whirling silver.

"Well, now, I don't know about that—"

"Only way you'll ever get it."

"Ain't how we planned it. Bray was to pay us off, then we'd turn Tod—the boy—loose."

"You're dealing with me not my brother. Far as I'm concerned you could take Tod and do what you damned pleased with him, but my brother wants him back, so that's how it's going to be—my way or not at all."

"You go rearing up on your hind legs like that and something for sure'll happen to that kid!"

"Still wouldn't get you the twenty-five thousand you're after—and that's what you and your partners are wanting. You figure to collect it, take me to where you're holding Tod and we'll make the swap."

Jake Cooney continued to frown and claw at his jaw, clearly uncertain as to the wisdom of such a course, while equally afraid to doubt the blunt words of the grim-faced man looking down at him.

"Ain't the way it was supposed to be," he mumbled.

"Maybe not, but it's the way it's going to be or no deal. Best you make up your mind to that."

Cooney's shoulders lifted and fell in a gesture of resignation. "All right," he said, "I reckon I ain't got no choice. You wait here, I'll get my horse."

Bray smiled. "Nope, I'll go along with you. Don't fancy letting you take a potshot at me soon's you're in the brush."

The outlaw paused, looked back. "Hell, I wouldn't try nothing like that."

Again Matt Bray smiled. "You forget I know you from a long time ago, Jake. And best you keep something in mind. One wrong move while we're riding and I'll blow your goddammed head off."

Cooney's face darkened. "Like hell you would! Sure fix that boy for good, was you to."

"He means nothing to me—only to my brother," Matt replied. "Doubt it'd make a difference to your friends, anyway. They'd still be ready to trade him for the money whether you were dead or not. . . . Let's go."

7

* * *

Jake Cooney's gray horse was picketed in a small, open patch of ground near the edge of the stream. Keeping behind the outlaw, Matt waited while the outlaw mounted, and then followed him back to the trail running alongside the creek. There Jake swung north, making it clear they would be going to Buffalo Crossing.

That's where they were holding Tod, Matt reckoned, most likely in some run-down shack at the edge of the settlement. Being the sort of town it was—or had been the last time he was there—it would be easy for the outlaws to carry out their plans. Law in Buffalo Crossing was practically nonexistent, and the sort that visited or inhabited the settlement believed in neither asking nor answering questions.

Further, none of the ranch hands from Rocking Chair ever patronized its establishments, preferring instead to go to Parsonville, thus reducing to zero the chances of someone seeing Tod Bray or hearing of his predicament, and reporting such to John.

"You living up in this neck of the woods nowadays?" Cooney asked conversationally, glancing back over his shoulder.

The question was merely to cover the outlaw's assessment of the situation and determine how

45

close a surveillance Matt was maintaining over him.

"Maybe," the tall rider replied noncommittally.

Jake shrugged, swore deeply as his horse, frightened by a bird exploding from the brush close by, shied violently. Then, "Sure never come to me that Tod was kin of your'n."

"You seem to know him."

"Not much. Run into him at the Prairie Rose a few times."

"Prairie Rose? What's that?"

"Saloon. In Buffalo Crossing."

Matt could not recall the place but he made no comment as they moved on. The morning air was growing steadily warmer now as the sun climbed toward its zenith.

"Who's partnering you in this?" he asked after a time.

Cooney grinned slyly. "Oh, couple a friends, maybe three. Reckon you'll know them."

"Expect I will," Bray said laconically.

The brush had begun to thin out and they were entering low hill country, covered with thin grass and dotted with an occasional cedar and clumps of bayonet yucca. The town would lie not far ahead, Matt recalled—just beyond a rocky hogback thrusting from the earth only a mile in the distance.

A thin spiral of smoke became visible a few minutes later, twisting up into the sky from the area on the far side of the ridge, and he guessed his memory was serving him correctly. The town would be crouched on the floor of a narrow valley, with Redbank Creek coursing through its center.

The place had grown some, but not much, Bray saw as he trailed the outlaw into the settlement's only street. Sundstrom's Hotel . . . Golden Eagle

General Store ... Gosta's Livery Stable ... a half-dozen rag-tag saloons, some nameless others with faded, illegible signs ... Dutch Alice's Restaurant ... Henry Arnot, Guns & Ammunition & Saddlery ... Caleb's Feed & Seed Store, which appeared to have gone out of business, for its doors were shut and had boards nailed across them. There once had been a print shop and a bank, but both had met the same fate as Caleb's and were now empty shells bleaching in the sunlight.

The entire dual line of buildings looked old and tired, their false fronts warped and weathered, their distinction gone. Dust lay hoof-deep in the narrow street, and there was no one in sight, it being that time of day when all preferred to remain indoors out of the heat.

Bray became aware of Cooney's turning off the main course and angling for an alleyway running past the livery stable. He saw the Prairie Rose then—a square, two-story structure sitting back from the other buildings, recalled that it had once been the residence of the town's leading citizen, evidently now deceased or departed for a settlement more to his liking.

A dozen horses stood at the hitchrack fronting the converted home, now painted in garish red and yellow, and the faint sound of a piano, over-ridden by the rumble of voices, was coming from its open doorway. A woman, watching their arrival with interest, was framed in one of the upper-floor windows, but by the time they reached the rack and pulled to a stop she had disappeared.

"Want you walking ahead of me all the way," Matt said as they tied their mounts alongside the others. Hanging the saddlebags containing the ransom over a shoulder, he hitched at the pistol on his hip. "What I said before still goes. You make a wrong move—"

Cooney shrugged. "I heard you. Just you tote along that there money."

Brushing his hat to the back of his head, the outlaw threw a glance to the window where the woman had been visible, and climbing the half-dozen steps leading up onto the broad porch, crossed and entered the building.

The walls of the rooms on the first floor of the house had been torn out to create a single, large area for the saloon. A bar had been built against the west end, complete with mirrors and shelves, but there were no bottles displayed and the mirrors were all cracked, with corners missing.

Tables and chairs were grouped around the room, and there was a long counter behind which a man wearing a green eyeshade and black satin sleeveguards was dealing cards to a solitary customer. A piano stood in a far corner, with a woman in a red and gold dress fingering the keys, while a scattering of patrons took their ease, listening, and several saloon girls looked on.

"Up them steps," Cooney said, pointing at a flight of stairs in the back of the saloon as he cut a path through the tables.

Bray, sweeping the faces, turned to him with a cold stare, said, "Take it slow and easy."

"Sure—but you best forget about that gun you're wearing."

"Maybe—"

They mounted the steps, gained the hallway on the second floor, which was dimly lit by a dust-streaked window at its far end. Cooney led the way past a half-dozen doors that turned off on either side, and halted before one near the center. Knotting a fist, he rapped on the scarred panel.

"It's me—Jake."

"Seen you coming," a voice from the inside answered. "What kind of a damn-fool stunt you pulling—bringing him here with you?"

Whoever was speaking had evidently recognized him, Matt realized, striving to place the voice. It was familiar but he couldn't pin it down.

"Wouldn't deal no other way."

"The hell. You was calling the shots."

"Sort of slipped up on me. Anyways, what difference does it make?"

"Plenty—and he's still packing his iron. You're running mighty short on brains, Jake."

Cooney swore angrily. "You wouldn't've done no different, was it a been you! Open the goddamn door!"

"Get his gun first—"

Jake turned, faced Bray, question in his eyes. Matt shook his head. Handing over his weapon was the last thing he had in mind to do.

"Not about to," he said.

"Can tell him he ain't seeing the kid alive again if he don't—money or no money," the voice from inside the room warned. "We ain't about to let him walk in here and shoot up the place."

Recognition of the speaker came to Matt Bray at that moment. "That Ben Fisk doing all the talking?"

Cooney nodded. "Sure is. You giving me your iron?"

He had no choice, Bray decided. Reaching down, he drew the forty-five from its holster and passed it to the outlaw. Downstairs the piano player had struck up a tune and there were shouts and stomping as dancing got under way.

"This deal better go through just like it's supposed to unless you want me looking for you the rest of your life," Matt said quietly. "Goes for Ben and whoever else is in there, too."

"Don't you fret none about it," Cooney replied, and again knocked on the door. "I got his gun. Open up."

The panel swung in. Jake Cooney drew aside and allowed Bray to move past him into the room—dim, shabby, with stained, curling wallpaper, worn rug, and scarred furniture.

Ben Fisk greeted him with a hard grin. Fisk was squat and husky, with red hair down to his shoulders and in need of cutting. His broad face was shining with sweat.

"Well, if it ain't old Six O'Clock! That the money in them saddlebags?"

Matt made no reply, his attention on a smaller, thinner counterpart of John Bray lounging in a chair near the lone window that graced the wall. The woman he'd noted there earlier was leaning against his shoulder. There was no mistaking Tod.

"Worked—slick as hog guts, just like you said it would, boy," Fisk said, grinning at Tod, and then pistol in one hand, he stepped forward and relieved Matt Bray of the saddlebags.

Tod stirred lazily, pulled the woman down onto his lap. "Told you he'd pay off," he said.

8

✷ ✷ ✷

Matt studied the boy coldly. Tod was part and parcel of the kidnapping. He guessed he should have expected it. After a time he shrugged.

"Might've known you'd be at the bottom of this."

Tod laughed. "Had to pry some cash out of Pa somehow. Was the best way I could think of—but I sure never figured on him bringing you in on it."

"He was scared there might be some trickery. Asked me to handle it so's he could be sure you'd be alive when it was all over."

"Sounds like Pa, for sure!" Tod said and shifted his glance to Fisk. "It all there, Ben?"

The outlaw had unbuckled the leather pouches and was thumbing through the packets of currency. "Looks like it—ain't done counting yet."

"It'll tally up to twenty-five thousand," Matt said, his voice heavy with disgust. "Don't worry about my brother shortchanging you."

"That's Pa, all right," Tod said, nodding. "Honest John Bray, you can call him!"

Matt placed his flat, cold gaze on Tod once again. "Your pa said you'd grown up, become a man. Guess it's something he wants to believe. Can see you're the same as always—even worse."

"I got the right to live the way I want—same as

you," Tod replied, and shifted his attention to the girl, giggling and squirming in his arms.

Bray glanced about, settled his gaze on the two other men in the room. One was Dave Agate, a hardcase from down along the border. The other was a younger, dark-faced rider he didn't know. Wearing crossed gunbelts, the man stood, arms folded, grinning at him from the center of the room.

"So you're that lead-chucker they call Six O'Clock," he said. "Been hoping to come across you someday, see if all them tales—"

"Forget it, Pete," Jake Cooney cut in. "You best stay clear of him if you want to keep on living."

The outlaw laughed. "Now, I ain't so sure he's all that good."

Bray turned away, faced Fisk. He'd run up against all too many Petes, had learned it was smart to ignore them unless forced to do otherwise.

"What's next, Ben?" he asked casually.

Fisk was buckling the saddlebags. "We're getting the hell out of here, that's what. Money was what we was wanting, and we've got it."

Bray nodded, glanced at Tod, now pushing the girl aside and coming to his feet. "And you?"

"I'm riding with them. Sure as hell ain't going back to the ranch—not with you still—"

"Reckon I can fix that for you," Pete drawled, patting the pistols on his hips. "Be a real pleasure—me taking him on."

"He ain't wearing no gun," Agate said, frowning.

"So what? Ain't nobody ever accused me of being kindhearted."

Matt, ignoring the young gunman, continued to

face Tod. "You sure you know what you're doing?"

"You're goddamn right I do! Been wanting to shove off on my own for quite a spell—just never had enough cash to do it. Now, with my share of the twenty-five thousand, I can start living the way I want—"

"High on the hog—" Dave Agate supplied, grinning.

"Yes, sir, high on the hog!"

"Your pa's figuring on you taking over the ranch, running it for him. And that girl, Karla, she's expecting you to marry her. You aim to just throw all that away?"

"Never did care nothing about raising cattle," Tod said, "and far as Karla goes, she's all right for a roll in the hay now and then, but I ain't about to saddle myself with her. . . . We pulling out right away, Ben?"

"Soon as we can get over to the livery stable and saddle up—"

"Suits me. I'll take the money, see to splitting it up first chance we get."

"Better let me keep looking after it," Fisk said and bucked his head at Pete. "You're so all-fired anxious to put a bullet in old Six O'Clock, go ahead, start doing it so's we can move out."

"Yes, sir—and it sure is going to be a real pleasure," the outlaw said, and reached for his guns.

Matt Bray reacted instantly. He rocked to one side, lunged forward. His big hands locked about Pete's wrists. The smirk disappeared from the gunman's narrow face as he yelled, the sound blending with a scream coming from the woman.

Pivoting on a heel, Matt swung Pete, badly off balance and all but falling, directly into Fisk and Jake Cooney. Both cursed, staggered back, Jake going to the floor. A gun blasted, filling the small room with a deafening report and swirling powder smoke.

Bray threw himself at Pete. The gunman, dazed, and on hands and knees, had both weapons out of their holsters. Matt reached for the nearest, endeavored to wrench it free. A booted foot smashed into his side, knocked him away before he could get a firm grip on the pistol.

Going over full length, he rolled frantically, seeking to avoid another blow to his ribs. There were several feet lashing at him—Tod's, Agate's and Ben Fisk's. He came up against the wall, reversed motion, managed to draw himself upright.

Tod was directly before him, eyes burning, features taut. Matt struck out with a balled fist, caught him solidly on the side of the head. As Tod went down he wheeled to meet Agate and Fisk, flinched as the latter slammed him across the head with the barrel of his pistol.

Stunned, Bray staggered back against the wall, aware of blood streaming down into his eyes, over his face. Shoulders against the wall, he fought to steady himself. He could hear the woman still screaming, hear shouts coming from the men, all vague shadows darting about in the haze of powder smoke.

"I got him—"

It was the voice of the eager little gunman, Pete.

"He's all mine—goddamn him!"

Ben Fisk yelled something. Tod Bray staggered

by, mouthing curses, and then came a blinding flash—a surge of pain in his head, and Matt felt himself pitching forward as darkness closed about him.

9

* * *

Matt Bray, pain sledgehammering inside his head, stirred slowly—froze. A long-observed instinct was cautioning him to have care; he might not be alone. His eyelids felt heavy, sticky, as he opened them. Blood, he realized, some of it still fresh, some dried. But it was nothing new. He was no stranger to having a bullet rip through him; pain and discomfort were to be expected. His sole consolation was that he was yet alive.

He was alone in the stifling, heat-trapped room. The outlaws and Tod were gone, evidently believing him dead. Matt sat up, explored the side of his head carefully with the tips of his fingers. More blood. He flinched at the slight pressure. Pete's bullet had cut a groove above his right ear. He'd dropped like an axed steer, no doubt, and the immediate rush of blood, combining with that released by Ben Fisk's blow with the pistol, had made it look as if he were finished.

But he wasn't—far from it. Anger running through him like wildfire, he struggled to his feet and staggered unsteadily across the room to the washstand. The china pitcher was half full of water, and pouring it all into the companion bowl, he lowered his face into it.

The sharp stinging brought a curse to his lips but he did not pull back, continued to bathe his

56

wounds until finally the pain had cleared away the mist clouding his brain and the stiffness was gone from his skin.

His injuries weren't too bad—deep cuts more than anything else, and the blood had almost stopped seeping from the gash above his ear. He crossed to the bed, pulled the slip from a pillow, and ripping a strip from it, wound it about his head as a bandage. Looking about, he located his hat and set it in place, cocking it to an angle where it all but completely covered the circle of white cloth.

Using the remainder of the cotton slip to clean and dry his face and neck, he turned to the window. There was nothing he could do about the crusted stains on his shirt other than remove and wash it—and he had no time for that.

He had no idea of how long he'd been unconscious. An hour or so, he reckoned. It was afternoon, but the street was still deserted, which could mean it was not far past midday. Tod and the outlaws he'd teamed up with to cheat his father could not have gotten too far in that short length of time—might possibly still be in town, downstairs in the saloon, perhaps. Having left him for dead, they would not be worrying about seeing him again.

Matt wheeled, crossed to the door, laid a hand on the knob. He hesitated, looked around hopefully. Jake Cooney had taken his gun from him; there was a chance the outlaw had thrown it aside rather than be bothered with its extra weight. It was wishful thinking; the weapon was nowhere to be seen. No matter—he had a spare in the saddlebags on his horse.

Opening the door, Bray stepped out into the

hall and quietly made his way to the stairs, then halted. Squatting so that he could have a full view of the activity below, he searched for Tod and the outlaws. They were not among the few patrons—nor did he see the woman who had been in the room. He doubted she would be of much help, anyway; they would have told her nothing of their plans.

The livery stable—that was his best bet. Fisk had said they would pull out as soon as they could get their horses; the hostler who took care of them might have heard them talking and could possibly give him some idea of the direction they had taken.

Grim, intent, looking neither to right nor left, Bray descended the stairs, stalked rigidly through the saloon and out to the hitchrack where the bay waited. Jerking the lines free, he went onto the saddle, taking a few moments to dig out the extra six-gun and holster it. Then, cutting about, he doubled back to the livery stable a short distance away.

To take advantage of a cooling breeze, the wide double-doors had been propped open. The place was totally quiet as Matt turned in, drew to a stop in the center of the runway of the low, shadowy building smelling of hay, leather, and droppings.

"Hostler!" he called when no one appeared.

Presently a squat figure, shirtless, wearing faded, stained overalls, run-down boots, and a battered, narrow-brimmed hat, emerged from one of the back stalls and shambled indifferently up to where Matt waited.

He opened his mouth to speak, frowned, eyes on the blood stains on Bray's shirt. Matt shrugged.

"What's the matter? Ain't you never seen a man that's been in a scrap before?"

The hostler brushed at a fly circling his face. "Something you're wanting, mister?"

"You Gosta?" he asked, recalling the name on the sign.

"Nope, he ain't here. Name's Jones."

"You been here all day?"

"Since the morning, early. Gosta had to go somewheres. Funeral, I think it was, over west of here."

"You'll do," Matt said. "Looking for some men. Friends of mine. Was supposed to meet them here. Would've been five in the bunch."

"Yeh, they was here," Jones said, cocking his head to one side and squinting. "Been a couple hours ago. Got their horses—leastwise four of them did. Was one fellow already riding."

"That'll be them. Which way did they ride out?"

Jones rubbed at the back of his neck with a grubby hand. "East—toward Texas."

Texas . . . It didn't make sense to Matt Bray. He would expect Fisk and the others, flush with cash, to head south for the Mexican border, where they would be safe from any repercussions. But then, he realized, they would not be in fear of such; he was dead as far as they knew, and by the time John Bray learned of what had happened they would be several hundred miles away in a broad land of little communication.

"Wasn't figuring they'd go east—"

"Well, that's what they done," Jones declared. "Aimed to haul up for the night in Sundown."

"That a town?"

"Yeh, about a half a day's ride, maybe a bit more."

"Obliged," Matt said abruptly, and swinging the gelding around, returned to the alley.

Reaching the street, he halted. He should let John know what had taken place, he supposed, but that would mean riding all the way back to the ranch, and then starting from there. It would cost him several hours—and like as not his brother would insist on mounting a posse from his hired hands to accompany him.

He'd do better without help—and losing that much time would be a mistake. Tod and the others would be taking it easy, confident there was no need for haste, and since they were only a couple of hours ahead of him, he might, by riding hard, overtake them. And telling John the truth about the son he set so much store by could wait. It would be difficult at best.

The throbbing of his wounds seemed to be intensifying. He should do something about them, he reckoned, but hunting up a doctor and wasting an hour or more being treated was also contrary to his desire. He'd do a bit of doctoring himself, and then, when it was all over—and if the slashes still bothered him—he'd find himself a sawbones and let him do his stuff.

Glancing about, Bray located a small saloon on the other side of the stable, and moving on, rode to it. Leaving the saddle, he entered the dark, shedlike structure that housed it, deserted except for one drowsy patron slumped over the crude counter that served as a bar. When the owner came from somewhere in the rear, Matt purchased a quart of whiskey and returned to his horse.

Hanging his hat on the saddlehorn, he unwound the makeshift bandage, grumbling when it stuck to the open wound, and saturated it with liquor. Then, taking a healthy swallow from the bottle to fortify himself, he put the bandage back in place.

It was as if he'd crowned himself with a band of fire, and for a long minute he stood motionless beside the big bay gelding, cursing vividly in a deep, steady monotone. Finally the burning subsided to a low stinging sensation, and carefully replacing his hat, he took another swig of the whiskey, stowed the bottle away in the saddlebags, and swung onto the bay.

As he doubled back to the street he saw Jones, the hostler, standing in the entrance to the livery stable, watching him curiously. Nodding curtly, Matt veered his horse onto the road leading eastward from the settlement and put him into a lope.

10

* * *

"You figure it's smart—us all riding in a bunch like this?" Jake Cooney wondered.

Fisk, to his left in the foragelike line, spat. "Don't see it making no difference."

The outlaw was in poor humor after finally turning the saddlebag of ransom money over to Bray. Tod had ragged and fretted him until, sick of the whining, he had complied.

"You fearing old Six O'Clock's ghost's a following us?" Pete asked with a laugh.

"No, ain't that. Reckon he's dead for sure," Cooney replied, not amused. "But if somebody goes into that there room and finds him laying there—"

"What'll they do?" Fisk demanded impatiently. "Nothing, plain nothing. Just be another saddle-bum that got hisself killed and's ready for planting in the boneyard."

"He ain't just another saddlebum," Cooney said, dissatisfied. "Plenty around who'll know who he is, even if they don't know he's kin to the kid's pa."

"Still think there ain't nothing nobody'll do about it," Fisk said angrily. "Anyway, if somebody took the notion, by the time they got around to doing something we'll be in Mexico.

Tod Bray, riding a bit apart from the others as

they made their way steadily southward across the rolling chaparral and snakeweed-covered plains, kneed his mount in nearer to Fisk.

"You aiming to hang around El Paso for a spell, Ben, or you crossing the river to the Mexican side and lining out for Chihuahua first off?"

"Ain't made up my mind. One thing's for sure, I'm taking it mighty easy from now on—and doing what I damn please. If I feel like it, I'll lay around El Paso. If'n I don't, I'll maybe cross the river to Paso del Norte, do my loafing there—or could be I'll take me a little trip up to Nogales. Good town, Nogales. Been told the prettiest senoritas in Mexico can be found there—and if it's gambling a man wants, he can suit his fancy. There's every kind there is. Fellow having a pile of money can do a lot of picking and choosing—women, gambling, or just living."

"That's for certain," Dave Agate agreed contentedly, shifting his weight on the saddle. "I ain't never had more'n fifty dollars in my pocket at one time in my whole life! Man starts out poor, he stays poor—unless he gets lucky. How much my share going to come to, Ben?"

"Just about four thousand dollars," Tod said before Fisk could answer.

"Godamighty!" Agate echoed in an awed tone. "Four thousand dollars! I ain't sure there's that much money in the world!"

"Well, there is and it's all yours," Bray said with a patronizing wave of his hand. "Every damn dollar of it."

Dave wagged his head. "Man, I'm sure going to have me a time spending it—

"You tie up with one of them saloon gals in El Paso and she'll help you get rid of it mighty fast,"

Cooney warned. "Been thinking about what I'll do with my share."

The outlaw paused, stared out across the vast flat, glittering in the hot sunlight. Far over to their right, two coyotes—jaws agape, tongues lolling, ragged tails extended stiffly—were trotting along in parallel but safe companionship with the five riders.

"Sort of like to buy myself a little piece of land somewheres," Jake continued. "About time to settle down and—"

"The hell," Pete cut in derisively. "You'll blow it on whiskey and women and bucking the tiger same as the rest of us. You ain't the settling-down kind no more'n we are, and six months from now you'll be plumb busted—just like always."

Jake shrugged, and eyes narrowed to cut down the glare, studied the coyotes. The sky was cloudless, and the heat as they pushed continually southward seemed to increase with each succeeding mile.

"Maybe," he murmured, "but I sure would like to do something right with it. Getting plenty tired of this here saddle."

"I sure ain't planning on settling down," Tod stated flatly. "I got me enough here to last for quite a spell—and I'm going to enjoy every minute of it—"

"On women and card playing," Pete added.

"Women mostly—"

"Where you figuring to light?"

"San Antone. Drummer told me that's a town where a fellow can have himself a time—and if he gets tired of what's going on there, it ain't but a hoot and a holler to the Mexican border—"

"Laredo," Agate said. "You know how far it is

to San Antone from here? Six hundred miles—and that's a hell of a ride."

Pete wiped at the sweat accumulated on his face with the back of a hand. "Ain't nothing in San Antone a fellow can't find in El Paso."

Tod shook his head. "Too close to home to suit me."

Pete stared at Bray. "Didn't figure that'd bother you none. Said your pa was all bunged up, and I fixed that long drink of water of an uncle of yours so's he won't be coming looking. Who else's around?"

"Nobody special. But every now and then some cowhand looking for work blows in that's been down El Paso way. Just could be one someday that'd remember me and say something to Pa."

"Still don't see what difference it'd make—"

"Maybe none, but I'll feel better if he don't ever hear about me again."

Pete pulled off his hat, ran his fingers through his sweat-soaked hair. "You know what? I think old Six O'Clock's got you spooked and you're fearing he ain't dead and'll be showing up again looking for you."

Jake Cooney nodded solemnly. "Maybe he's got a right. Fact is I'd feel a lot better if I'd seen him getting buried. He's a hard one to kill off—Ben there'll back me up on that."

"Been a few tried doing it before, all right," Fisk admitted, leaning forward on his saddle to ease his muscles. He had been unusually quiet for some time, as if wrapped in deep thought.

"Well, it's been done this time—can bet your bottom dollar on that!" Pete said, anger in his tone. "I don't stand no six foot away from a man and miss. You all seen him go down—bleeding like a stuck hog. Must've blowed half his damned head off."

"Yeh, I seen it all right," Cooney said.

"Then maybe you're believing in spooks like the Indians do."

Jake's shoulders stirred as he looked off in the direction of the two coyotes. They had veered in their course, were now angling toward a stretch of low, white sand hills to the southwest.

"Like I told you," he said doggedly, "I'd feel a powerful lot better if I'd seen him getting dirt throwed in his face—but I reckon you did finish him for sure. . . . Ain't heard you say what you're doing with your share of the cash."

"Got real big plans," Pete replied. "First off I'm buying me some new duds—the fancy black kind with silver buttons. And I'm getting myself the best pair of boots I can find, ones with a lot of pretty stitching on the legs. Seen a pair a fellow was wearing up in Ellsworth once. Claimed he paid fifty dollars for them. I'm aiming to pay a hundred for mine.

"Buying myself a new horse, too, one of them big yellow-looking animals with the white mane and tail. Hear there's some rancher down in Mexico that raises them. Can use a new pair of irons while I'm fixing up, along with all that other stuff. Think I'll get silver-plated ones, with a lot of engraving on the barrel and with pearl handles."

"You're really duding up!" Dave Agate observed. "Anything else?"

"Aim to just start riding, visiting all them big towns I've heard tell about. Maybe I'll even get on a stagecoach and go clean back East to New York."

"You decide to do that, look me up in San Antone and I'll side along with you," Tod said. "Always did want to see what them big towns look like."

Ben Fisk swiped at the sweat on his face. He shifted wearily. "Before you two get all your money spent, maybe we best pull up over there by that tree and do the divvying," he drawled. "Can't see no point in holding off till we get to El Paso. There's a couple of towns 'tween here and there and I don't aim to be walking around with my pockets empty."

Tod frowned. "I'd rather wait. Can give you a couple of dollars if you're busted."

"I am—and so are all the rest of us," the outlaw said. "Just you toss me them saddlebags and I'll parcel out what we each got coming."

"Said no," Bray replied stubbornly, "and I reckon I got the say-so. This here ransom was my idea. Could even say it's my money since it come from my pa."

Fisk settled his small, hard eyes, reddened by dust and the relentless sun, on Bray. "You ain't hatching up some scheme to duck out on the boys and me when we get to El Paso—keep it all for yourself, are you?"

"Yeh, I'm wondering about that, too," Dave Agate said. "Just could be he's got some friends waiting there to give him a hand and cut us out of what we got coming."

"That ain't so!" Tod shouted. The back and front and the areas below the armpits of his shirt were dark from sweat, and the skin of his face had a wet shine. "I'm splitting it up just like we planned—ten thousand for me, because it was my idea—the rest going to you."

"That's less'n four thousand a piece," Fisk said

thoughtfully. "Don't hardly seem a fair split to me, does it to you boys?"

"Its kind of little," Pete agreed.

"Well, if it wasn't for me you'd be getting nothing—don't you be forgetting that!" Tod said, his voice rising. "You'd all still be hanging around the Prairie Rose or some other stinking saloon, flat busted!"

"Maybe not," Ben Fisk said dryly. "I lived thirty-five years before I run into you, boy, and there's been a few times when my poke was full. If you hadn't come along with your scheme to euchre your pa, something else would've turned up. Now, just pass me them saddlebags so's I can get on with it."

"No, I'm going to hold off till—"

"I reckon we'll just take it all, then," Fisk said, reaching for his pistol.

Tod drew back in alarm, his eyes widening, his skin losing its color. He endeavored to wheel away. Fisk fired at point-blank range.

Tod Bray jolted as the heavy bullet drove into his chest. He rocked back as his horse shied in a tight circle, hung briefly in rigid, shocked silence, and then fell to the hot sand.

Fisk, calmly holstering his weapon, moved in close to the nervous buckskin. Leaning over, he took up the leather pouches, hung them across his own saddle.

"Makes the divvying a little better—four ways instead of five," he said, cutting back to where the others were waiting. "He wasn't much of a partner, anyways."

"That's for sure," Pete agreed as they rode on.

11

* * *

Matt Bray halted on the crest of a hill, eyes on the settlement of Sundown below. The town was clustered in the center of a wide but shallow bowl in the prairie. There were many trees, a small shimmering pond of dark water, and grass was plentiful. Off in the distance he could see other, smaller, islands of green scattered across the brown land. Homesteaders, he assumed, and possibly a few small ranchers.

Turning, he glanced to the west. The sun was gone and it would be dark in another hour or so. He had ridden his horse hard to reach the settlement before nightfall—and he had made it. Tod and his outlaw friends would be there, planning no doubt to lie over until morning. They had a surprise coming, an unpleasant one.

Riding off the hill, Bray descended the gentle slope and reached the end of the single street leading into the town. Swinging onto it, he followed its dusty course to the collection of buildings and houses—a dozen and a half at most—rising to irregular heights around a plaza, in the center of which was a horse trough shaded by a lone cottonwood tree.

Pulling to a stop there, Matt let the bay slake his thirst while he scoured the encircling structures with narrowed eyes. There were no horses in

sight, and Sundown appeared deserted except for
the faces he could see at several windows watching
him with the suspicion local residents reserve for
strangers.

The principal building, the general store, bore
a sign above its entrance with the single word, GAR-
RISON'S. The town's one saloon adjoined it, and
was evidently run in conjunction with it. Elsewhere he noted a feed and seed store, a butcher
shop, a combination bakery and restaurant, a
hardware store, a harness and farm equipment
dealer, a livery stable and blacksmith, and a few
other miscellaneous establishments—none of which
appeared to be overly prosperous.

Tod and the outlaws, after spending most of
the hot day riding over the plains between Buffalo
Crossing and the settlement, would most likely be
in the saloon. Their horses probably had been
stabled for the night, which would account for
their not being in evidence.

Swinging the bay away from the trough, Bray
slanted across the plaza to the rack fronting the
saloon. Dismounting, aware of the covert attention still being accorded him, he wrapped the
gelding's lines about the crossbar and stepped up
onto the building's small landing. The saloon, he
saw then, was entered by way of the general store,
and without further delay he moved on through
the open doorway and into the square structure,
with its walls of shelves and counters.

A slender but well-formed woman with dark
hair gathered in a bun at the nape of her neck,
steady gray-blue eyes, and skin the color of cream,
came forward out of the shadows in the back of
the room to meet him. She had not yet lit a lamp
against the coming night and there was a softness

to everything around her in the confines of the crowded store.

"I'm Marcie Garrison," she said, taking in his size with a smile as she extended her hand. "Did you come about the lawman job?"

There had been few women in Matt Bray's life since Lilah—none that held his interest for more than an hour or so—but there was something about this one that stirred him despite the long, hot ride that had left him dusty and tired.

He shook his head. "No. Looking for five men. Figured they might be in the saloon."

Disappointment slacked the woman's even features. She gestured to an open archway leading into the adjoining area.

"There's no one in there—you can see for yourself."

Bray glanced into the empty room. Its only furniture consisted of a small counter, behind which was a shelf of bottles and glasses, and a half-dozen tables with chairs. It was deserted as she had said. He came back to her.

"Maybe you've seen them. Five men. Would've rode in from the west—an hour or so ago."

Marcie Garrison said, "No, there's been nobody come in but you."

Bray gave that thought. The outlaws and Tod would have had to pass by way of the settlement—and the chances they would stop here, layover, were a hundred to one.

"Looked like this was the only saloon in town; that right?"

The woman nodded. "No others within fifty miles in any direction. If they came this way, they'd be here."

Matt was not convinced they weren't. They

could have brought a supply of liquor with them, could be keeping out of sight somewhere in the town while they rested and enjoyed their whiskey.

"I'm obliged to you, ma'am," he said, touching the brim of his hat as he turned for the door.

"You're welcome," Marcie replied with a smile. "Come again."

Bray hesitated, glanced back at her. "Expect I'll do that," he said, and returned to the hitchrack.

Mounting the gelding, he doubled back across the plaza for the livery stable. He'd inquire there. An elderly man, squatting on his heels in the coolness of the stable's runway, shoulders to a wall, and with a cigar butt clenched between his teeth, looked up as Matt pulled to a halt in the entrance.

"Nope, ain't seen nobody ride in today other'n you," he said in reply to Bray's question.

"It'd be a long chance they didn't stop. Could they've gone through without you noticing them?"

"Ain't likely. Only one road in and one road out. They'd go through here no matter where they was heading, and I sure would've seen them. Why you looking for them? You the law?"

"No, just got some business to settle with them."

"Well, they sure ain't been here. This place is called Sundown—you sure you've got the right town?"

A slow anger was building within Matt Bray—a deep suspicion that he had been deliberately tricked, misled.

"Sundown's right. Beginning to think I was told wrong."

"Expect you was, friend. Ain't been five men ride into here in a bunch in a month of Sundays—

unless you count that gang from over Kansas way that's been giving us trouble. About a dozen of them bastards. Raise hell something fierce—just take over the place. I was sort of hoping you was coming to take over the lawing job."

"Woman over in the store seemed to think so, too. Town looks big enough to me to have its own marshal."

"Did—once. Fellow by the name of Lincoln—same as old Abe. Went and got hisself killed first time them jayhawkers showed up. They been hoorawing us ever since." The stableman hesitated, removed the cigar butt from between his teeth, and leaned forward. "Say, you wouldn't be interested in the job, would you?"

Matt shook his head. "No, afraid not. Got my own problems."

He had been sent on a wild-goose chase—and intentionally, he was convinced of that now. The hostler in Buffalo Crossing—Jones—had lied to him. For what reason, it was hard to understand, but he had.

There was nothing to do but return, look up Jones, and force the man to tell the truth. Bray swore under his breath; the bay, pressed hard to reach Sundown, was in no condition to make the trip back without feed and rest. He'd have to wait until morning.

"There a place around here where a man can get a room for the night?" he asked resignedly.

The stableman pointed at the general store with a stubby finger. "Mrs. Garrison. She's got a couple rooms out back of her place she rents to pilgrims. Can eat there, too. if you ain't of a mind to take your meal at the restaurant."

Bray nodded, came off the saddle. Then, "You

said Mrs. Garrison—she got a husband?" He'd noticed no one else around.

"Had. Lost him in the war."

"I see. You look after my horse? Like him grained and rubbed down."

"Sure. Boy of mine'll be along pretty soon and I'll put him at it. Cost you a dollar."

Matt tossed a silver coin to the old man, who caught it, tucked it into a pocket in his vest. "Expect you'll be wanting him in the morning."

"Early—"

"He'll be ready and waiting."

Bray, simmering at the thought of the hot, useless ride he'd been tricked into making, head throbbing anew now from his wounds, turned on a heel and started for the Widow Garrison's store and a room where he could clean up and then stretch out for a while. By the time he made it back to Buffalo Crossing, the outlaws and Tod would have a full day's lead on him—possibly more. Jones, the hostler, was going to have some explaining to—

"There come some of them jayhawkers now!"

12

$\times$ $\times$ $\times$

The livery stable man's words registered dully
on Matt Bray's consciousness, had no immediate
meaning as he strode rigidly, anger whipping
through him, toward Garrison's store. And then as
half a dozen riders rushed past—one so close that a
saddle stirrup grazed him, while a cloud of choking dust swirled over him—he realized what had
been said.

The bunch of hardcases from Kansas—jayhawkers, the old man had called them, falling back on
the term current during the war. Bray halted, all
the frustration and teeming wrath and bitterness
within his lanky frame surfacing abruptly.

"What the hell's the matter with you?" he
snarled.

The riders, almost to the rack in front of the
saloon, pulled their horses to a sliding stop,
wheeled.

"Who's wanting to know?" a slim, dark man in
the group demanded instantly, dropping from his
saddle.

"I'm betting he's the new john-law here," another said, resting a forearm on the horn and leaning forward. "He's sure a high one. Going to raise
a lot of dust when he falls."

An older rider, with a sweeping mustache and
square-cut beard, nodded sagely. "Reckon we best

75

start in right now showing him who owns this here burg."

The slim dark man waved him and the others back. "This'n here's mine. You all didn't let me in on the fun last time."

A bleak, humorless smile pulled at Matt Bray's lips as he folded his arms across his chest. Beyond the Kansans he could see Marcie Garrison, features taut, standing in the doorway of her store. Other faces were peering out at him from windows.

"Best you climb back on your horse and ride out, friend," he said coldly. "Goes for all of you. I'm not looking for trouble, but I just made a long ride for nothing and I ain't feeling charitable."

"Charitable?" the slim rider echoed. "You all hear that? He ain't charitable—what the hell's that mean?"

"Same as saying he don't want to hurt you none, Charlie," the bearded man explained.

"Well, now, that's real nice of him—but I reckon I ain't charitable none myself. High-pockets, if you can use that hogleg you're packing, you best get at it."

Bray shook his head. "Telling you for the last time, move on," he said in a winter-dry voice.

His hard, set face had a chiseled look, and there was an emptiness in his pale eyes. His tall shape looming darkly in the failing light, he appeared to be at absolute ease, yet there was a coiled look to him, like a rattlesnake poised to strike.

Charlie let his hands fall to his sides. His shoulders came forward slightly. "You're talking to the wrong cowboy, mister," he said quietly, and made a stab for the pistol on his hip.

Bray's bullet drove the man back and down before he could clear leather with his weapon. The bearded oldster yelled, came half about. It was a fatal move, though probably an innocent gesture of surprise. Matt Bray's second bullet, triggered only a breath after the first, ripped into him, knocked him from his shying horse.

Bray stood motionless in the seemingly frozen moments of time that followed. Powder smoke and dust, raised by the churning hoofs of the nervous horses, were drifting lazily about him, and somewhere along the street a dog, startled by the echoing gunshots, was barking frantically. And then from among the Kansans came an awed voice.

"Good God, he's killed Charlie and Ed—"

The line of Bray's shoulders softened, broke. He lowered his gun, slid it back into its holster.

"Unless some of the rest of you aim to try your luck, load them up and get out of here."

There was no affirmative response, and immediately two of the riders dismounted, hurriedly lifted their dead partners and hung them across the saddles of their horses. Equally quickly they went back onto their mounts, and without meeting the tall man's cold, level gaze, wheeled and rode out of the plaza.

Matt waited until they had disappeared into the closing darkness, and then shrugging, resumed his walk toward Garrison's store. Around him doors were coming open, people were running into the street, shouting congratulations at him. He felt a hand clap him on the shoulder, turned. It was the livery stable owner.

"You sure fixed them, mister! That Charlie—he

was the worst of the lot! They won't be coming back here no more!"

"We're sure obliged to you!" another man stated, reaching for Matt's hand and shaking it violently. "They been running us ragged ever since Tom Lincoln got killed."

Bray came to a halt at the landing in front of Garrison's. Removing his hat, and forgetting the stained bandage it had concealed, he brushed at the sweat on his forehead. He was not thinking of the town's problems with the Kansas outlaws when he shot it out with them, was only defending himself and exorcising a measure of the anger that filled him. But it pleased him that the killings were just and for good purpose; taking any man's life was never an occasion for satisfaction, regardless of cause.

"Ain't there some way we can pay you for what you done?"

Matt did not see who asked the question, but he shook his head. "All I'm wanting is a room to spend the night, and a bite to eat. Got to be on my way, come morning."

A groan went through the crowd gathered before him. "We was hoping you'd take on the marshal's job," someone said. A chorus of approval followed.

"Appreciate the offer, but I've got other business," Bray said, and turned to Marcie Garrison. "Was told I could rent a room here and take supper."

"You can," she said, smiling, and stepped back so that he could enter. "Rest of you go on into the saloon. Tom, you do the bartending. This is a day to celebrate, so the drinks are on the house."

Another burst of yells went up as Marcie

wheeled around, motioning at Matt to follow, and led him through the back of the store to where she maintained living quarters. Pointing to a chair in the kitchen, she told him to be seated.

"Supper's about ready," she said, "but first I want to change that bandage around your head. You can clean up then while I set the table—that is, unless you want to go in with the others, do some drinking."

Bray gave that but a moments thought. "That can wait," he said.

13

* * *

Shortly after four o'clock that next morning Matt Bray was up and pulling on his clothes. He had enjoyed a good night's rest in the comfortable room made available to him by Marcie Garrison, and while he was expected to remain for breakfast, he felt it was important that he return to Buffalo Crossing and get on the trail of Tod and his outlaw friends as soon as possible.

The previous evening had been more than pleasant. The people of Sundown could not do enough for him in showing their gratitude. In shooting down two of the Kansas outlaws who had been harassing the town, he had removed a threat to their otherwise peaceful way of life, and they were insistent in showing their appreciation. He dared not mention a need for anything, because if it was available, it was immediately his—and his money had no value.

Marcie Garrison did not permit herself to be outdone by her fellow Sundowners. Not only did she attend to his head wounds, applying some sort of healing salve and a clean bandage, but she also served up a fine supper, after which she washed and pressed his shirt so that his appearance might be less grim.

They joined the others in the saloon after that, and then later when the festivities had come to an end, they retired to the fenced yard behind the house, and there beneath the dark, arching canopy of the star-filled sky, they sat and talked of their lives, of what had been and what they hoped for.

To Matt Bray and Marcie it was a time of release, of catharsis. Lonely, withdrawn from life, each for different reasons, they had quickly discovered common ground upon which to base understanding. Thus words flowed freely, leaving each regretful when the time came to call a halt and seek out their respective beds.

Matt arose early the next morning and made his preparations to leave quietly, pausing in the kitchen to leave a half eagle on the table as pay for his room and board, and then decided it was best to forgo doing so for fear of offending her.

He had already paid—Mathewson the livery stable owner, whose name he'd learned the previous evening—for the care of the bay. Thus when he entered the squat structure, dimly lit by a single lantern hanging in the runway, he avoided awakening the old man, and seeking out his horse, saddled and bridled him. Leading the big gelding to the street, he mounted and struck west.

When he reached the top of the hill where earlier he'd had his initial glimpse of the settlement, Matt paused, looked back. For the first time in his life he was finding it difficult to leave a town. He'd made friends in Sundown despite the brevity of his stay. And Marcie Garrison . . . she had brought alive something within him that was changing his outlook on life.

He'd like one day to return to Sundown, and perhaps he would. The town's reluctance to let him go had been no greater than his desire to remain—but he had a task to perform, one of honor, which he deemed best not to reveal, particularly to Marcie. When it was over, and if he were still alive, he just might go back.

Bray didn't push the bay, in fine fettle after a night's rest and feeding, knowing that the trip to Buffalo Crossing would be only the beginning of the day's work. As soon as he determined the true direction which Tod and the outlaws had taken, he would set out in pursuit. They had a long start on him, but it wouldn't matter; he'd overtake them eventually.

It was late in the morning when he reached the settlement on Redbank Creek. He rode direct to the livery stable, halted at the rack, and dismounting, went inside. His anger at being lied to was now a cold, restrained force that made his hard-cornered features even more angular. As he entered the stable, he pitched his wide shoulders aggressively forward—like some wild animal preparing to spring.

A boy came out of the room that apparently served as an office for the stable owner, stopped, and stared at him.

"Where's Jones?" Matt snapped.

The boy jerked a thumb toward the Prairie Rose. "In there, I reckon—"

Bray wheeled, and with the bay trailing along behind him, walked the short distance to the saloon. A number of people were on the street, and many paused to glance his way, struck not only by his towering figure but by the threatening look of him as he strode purposefully through the dust.

Entering the structure, Matt halted a few steps inside the cluttered room. There were only a half-dozen patrons and a couple of the gaily clad girls in attendance, and he located Jones at once. The hostler was sitting at one of the back tables with two men, laughing and talking, a bottle of whiskey before them.

Matt crossed the length of the saloon to the party. Without comment or preliminaries of any sort, he reached out, grasped Jones by the shirt front. Yanking the man to his feet, Bray spun him about and slammed him hard against the wall.

A yell of protest went up from the hostler's two friends, and both sprang erect. Ignoring them, Bray caught Jones with a hard right to the belly as the man rebounded from impact against the thick, wooden paneling, then drove his left into the jaw as Jones buckled forward with an explosion of breath.

The handful of patrons in the Prairie Rose had come to startled attention and were beginning to gravitate toward the disturbance. One of the men with Jones, pushing away from the table, grabbed Bray by the arm.

"What the hell—" he began and staggered back as Matt struck him a stinging blow across the face.

Jones, gasping, sagged against the wall. He shook his head in an attempt to clear his reeling senses. Bray slapped him smartly.

"That's for lying to me," he ground out in a savage voice, and slapped the man again.

Abruptly Matt staggered. Jones' two friends were cutting themselves in. He felt the arms of one go about his waist, and braced himself to support the man's weight. A fist came from somewhere, caught him on the jaw. It was a glancing blow, hardly felt. He swore, lunged to one side, breaking the grip of the man struggling to drag him off his feet.

"Keep out of this!" he snarled, and threw the man clinging to him back against the table, upsetting it as they both hit the floor in a tangle of legs and arms.

Bray winced as a fist again found its target, this time on the side of his head. He wheeled, anger roaring through him, and with a hard shove sent the man stumbling into the small knot of spectators gathered nearby. Then, sucking deep for wind, sweat pouring off him, he turned back to Jones. Seizing the hostler again by the shirt front, he jerked him upright.

"I want straight talk from you!" he shouted. "Or else I—"

"Leave him be!" a voice came at him from the group of bystanders. "You done near killed him already!"

The scrape of heels brought Matt around. He rocked to one side as a chair smashed down upon him. He took the blow on his shoulders, pivoted to face three men—vague, hunched shapes, moving fast, converging on him.

Bray flattened himself against the wall, features suddenly bleak, eyes narrowed to mere slits. His hand swept low, came up with the pistol that hung at his hip. He struck out—a short, arching blow. The barrel of the weapon laid a red welt across the forehead of the man nearest him, sent him stumbling back, mouth flared. The pair siding him paused uncertainly, retreated.

"Between me and Jones," Matt snapped, sucking deep for wind. "Keep out of it unless you're looking for some real trouble!"

His brittle glance touched the crowd, confirming the warning, and then he swung to Jones. The hostler had regained his scattered senses, now tried to pull away. He froze as Matt put the muzzle of his pistol to his throat.

"What—what do you want?"

"Goddamn you—you lied to me—sent me riding clear to Sundown and back for nothing!" Bray said, his voice again low and controlled.

Jones, breathing noisily, hands shaking badly, wagged his head. "I—I didn't know it was all that important—"

"Why'd you lie?" Matt demanded roughly. "They tell you to?"

The bystanders had now drawn well back, were content to do no more than listen and watch. The man Bray had buffaloed was holding a handkerchief to the bleeding wound on his forehead, and the ones he'd knocked aside were on their feet but apparently no longer anxious to mix in.

"They told me to tell anybody asking—not just you—anybody."

"Tell what?"

"That they was heading east, toward Texas. Give me ten dollars to—"

"Which way did they go?"

"South."

"You better be damn sure this time! You send me off on a snipe hunt again and I'll come back and blow your lying head off!"

Jones slumped against the wall. "It's the God's truth, mister. They went south—leastwise that's the way they was riding when they left here."

South—for the border. That made sense. Matt nodded slowly, holstered his gun. Tod and the outlaws would figure they'd be safe across the line should anyone set out after them—but just who that would be, Matt could not understand. They had left him for dead, thus they'd have no need to

fear him, and considerable time would elapse before his brother John grew suspicious at Tod's
failure to return home and he sent someone to in-
vestigate. . . . It was Ben Fisk's doing, he decided,
finally. Ben was the careful sort, and he was taking precautions.

Moving forward, Bray pushed the overturned
table aside, kicked a chair out of his way. The
crowd fell back, clearing a path for him as they
gave way before his towering figure.

"Sure never figured to cause you no trouble,
mister," Jones mumbled. "Just didn't see nothing
wrong in doing what they asked."

Matt threw a hard glance to the hostler. "Man
lies, he best figure to take what's coming to him
when he gets caught. Who gave the ten dollars to
you?"

"Was the redheaded fellow—"

Ben Fisk. He was right. The outlaw was taking
no chances, was covering his trail—or trying to.

Matt moved on, heading for the door, ignoring
the half-angry, half-fearful glances turned on him
by the now sizable group gathered in the saloon.
Reaching the door, he halted, placed his winter-
cold glance on Jones once more.

"Warning you again—if you're lying—"

"I ain't, mister! I sure ain't!" the hostler replied
hurriedly. "They rode south."

Bray nodded curtly, and stepping out onto the
porch of the Prairie Rose, crossed to where the
bay was standing. Swinging up onto the saddle, he
cut back to the street and pointed south.

14

* * *

There could be no following of tracks on the road that led from Buffalo Crossing. A well-used route, it was a welter of hoof prints and wagon-wheel tire marks, and Matt Bray wasted no time endeavoring to ferret out those left by Tod and the outlaws. He could only bear south, convinced they would be headed for the border and the twin settlements that lay along it—El Paso on the American side, Paso del Norte on the Mexican.

The heat had risen gradually as the day grew older, and by noon he was feeling its full force. But Bray was a man accustomed to the heat and it bothered him little. His chief concern was for the bay, and while he held the horse to a good pace, he was careful not to allow the big gelding to overdo.

Nor did he entirely ignore the hoof prints in the road. The outlaws could have a change of mind, cut off, and take a different direction. It would be like Ben Fisk, an old hand at the game of avoiding pursuit, to do so. Matt felt he could take nothing for granted.

Around the middle of the afternoon he encountered a family moving north in a canvas-covered farm wagon, and halting them, asked for information concerning five riders they might have seen. The driver, an elderly man in a black, flat-crowned

87

hat, collarless shirt buttoned at the throat, scratched at his ragged beard, finally shook his head.

"Seen two fellows," he said. "Sure weren't no five in the bunch. One was riding a black, the other a sorrel.

Bray had no idea what color horses the outlaws and Tod had; he'd seen only the one being forked by Jake Cooney, but he doubted the pair were members of the party he was trailing. They'd not be separating as yet; perhaps they'd split up at the first town en route—a place called Las Cruces, but it was still a day's ride away.

"How long've you been on this road?" Matt asked, taking an extra few minutes to rest and cool the bay.

"Only since yesterday morning. Come in from Arizona way."

It would seem the pilgrim should have noticed the outlaws, since he was on the same road as Tod and the others—and there was no alternate route; but, of course, the farmer and his family could have pulled off at some time to make camp and rest, allowing the outlaws to pass by unseen.

"You hear of anybody hiring on men?" the bearded man asked in a hopeful voice.

Bray shook his head. "Can't think of anybody offhand. Plenty of ranches on farther north. Reckon you can find work on one of them if you're not particular what you do."

"I ain't," the pilgrim said flatly. "Things just petered out for me in Arizona and I sure got to find me a job somewheres. . . . Say, you ain't got some tobacco you could spare, have you?"

Matt twisted about, dug into his saddlebags,

and procured the extra sack of Bull Durham he was carrying. He held it up for the man to see.

"This do?"

"Sure will!" the pilgrim replied, reaching out eagerly. "Ain't no great shakes for chewing, but it'll be better'n nothing. Like somebody said, man begging can't be choosey."

Matt smiled, tossed the tobacco to the man, who caught it, then hesitated, frowning.

"I can't even scrape up a copper to pay—"

"Forget it," Bray said, and nodding to the slack-faced, sun-bonneted woman on the seat beside the pilgrim, and the cluster of small children peering out from the depths of the canvas arch behind the couple, he rode on.

The heat increased as the land flattened into endless, sandy plains studded with chaparral, cholla cactus, round clumps of snakeweed, and occasional large mounds of mesquite. The view was far-reaching, open except for the far-distant hills miles to his right, and the dark, ragged-rimmed Organ Mountains barely visible ahead.

But there was little point in straining his eyes searching the horizon for signs of the party. They had too great a lead on him—almost a full day and night—if they had not halted. He could only make certain he was on the right trail.

An hour later confirmation came. The road, which had been maintaining a due-south course, now began to veer toward a line of dark-faced bluffs to the west. It would circle the formations, Matt recalled, to touch a settlement, the name of which he could not remember, that lay in that area.

As he was probing his mind for the name he noticed the sudden appearance of hoof prints on the shoulder of the road and drew up abruptly. Dropping from the saddle, he squatted, examined the marks both on the edge of the traveled path and in the loose sand off to the side.

A grunt of satisfaction came from his throat. It was the outlaw party. The definite prints of five horses moving an arm's length apart were there. Ben Fisk and the others, not wanting to lose time by following the circuitous route, were striking out across country. Any doubts he might have had were now erased.

Going back onto the bay, Matt cut down off the slightly higher roadbed and began to follow the tracks. They were plain in the crusted surface of the flat, and for a time he traveled at a good pace. Then, in a broad strip of loose rock the marks disappeared and he was forced to continue without guidance.

But he needed no hoof prints to blaze his way. It was clear the outlaws had not separated and were bearing straight for the border. They were in a land where settlements were few—only Buffalo Crossing well to the north, the one he could not remember the name of to the west, and a place commonly called Cruces on the yonder side of the Organs, a half day's ride ahead. The nearest Texas town was a good two hundred miles east.

The outlaws would be tired, probably in need of water and supplies—and the only place within immediate reach where such were available was Cruces. Bray grinned tightly, wiped at the sweat misting his eyes. He had them now; he need only push on, and if luck was with him, he'd find them in Cruces. If they had not lain over, rested a bit as expected, he had but to continue on to El Paso and the border, less than forty miles beyond.

Bray pulled off his hat, again sleeved away the accumulated sweat. He still wore the bandage Marcie Garrison, who had asked no questions as to the cause of his wounds, had applied that night in Sundown. Evidently she had considered it his business, and that if he had felt it necessary, he would have explained. . . . Marcie Garrison was a fine woman, he had to admit that.

He'd thought little of his injuries, being troubled only slightly by them thanks to Marcie's healing salve, but now salty moisture trapped under the strip of cloth was causing a burning sensation that was annoying, and he considered removing the bandage. He decided against it, however, and after a time replaced his hat, setting it at an angle to avoid pressure on the cuts.

He would be needing Cruces and its conveniences, too, before long, he realized. His canteen was getting low and there was only a small amount of food in his grub sack. He should have restocked in Buffalo Crossing, but he'd pulled out in such haste that it had slipped his mind. But it was of no consequence; he'd had a big meal in Sundown the night before, and going a full twenty-four hours or better with little or no food would not be a new experience.

Matt glanced toward the sun. Still a few hours until it set. He would have to make up his mind whether to pull off and make camp for the night, or continue on to Cruces. He'd saved the bay as much as possible, and doubtless the big gelding could make it on into the settlement if allowed to choose his own pace.

Matt Bray's attention shifted, idly centered on a half-dozen vultures circling low not too far ahead. Something was attracting the big, broad-winged scavengers. A steer, perhaps? He discarded that assumption. There were no ranches in that particular area—a land of sand, weeds, cactus, and no water. An animal of some sort—a coyote or a fox—

He saw a horse several minutes later. It was standing off to his right a short distance from the line he was following. Head down, hip slacked, it appeared to have been there for some time. And then Bray caught sight of a dark shape sprawled in the weeds close by the horse. It took only a quick glance to see that it was a man.

Matt threw a hurried look about. Apaches were known to haunt that part of the country on occasion. This could be some of their work, although it was unlikely they would abandon a victim's horse. He saw no signs of anyone, Indian or otherwise, and raking the bay with his spurs, rode to where the crumpled figure lay.

Coming off the gelding, he again made a sweeping, circular examination of the land, and was reassured by its complete emptiness. Crossing to the body, he knelt beside it, and rolled it over. His jaw tightened and a curse slipped from his lips. It was Tod.

15

✷ ✷ ✷

Tod had been shot in the chest at close range, Matt saw. He was probably dead before he fell from his saddle, and it looked as if he'd made no attempt to defend himself, thus indicating the bullet had been unexpected. And he had been robbed; he had no money on him.

The answer was simple. Ben Fisk and the others had killed Tod for his share of the ransom. Twenty-five thousand dollars split four ways was better than split five ways, to their way of figuring.

Tod had been a fool—he should have been on the alert for just such a move on their part. With so much cash at stake, men like Fisk and Cooney and the others would not hesitate to do whatever was necessary to claim it all. Tod had simply overmatched himself in choosing partners in crime; among them he was as a lamb consorting with wolves. Likely they had not intended to give him his share from the very start.

Matt rose, glanced about. He would have to take Tod back to Rocking Chair. He couldn't bury him there on the mesa, nor could he just leave him—and it was too late to start back. Best thing would be to move over to a stand of mesquite he could see off to his right, make a night camp, and start for the ranch early in the morning. He could forget now all hope of overtaking the outlaws in Cruces; he'd have to plan on trailing them on into El Paso or possibly across the river to Paso del Norte.

Unrolling his blanket, Matt wrapped it about the boy's lifeless body, and loading it on the horse still waiting close by patiently, moved to the mesquite, his mind already disliking the thought of having to break the news of Tod's death to John.

Blind to all his faults, as men are wont to be when their offspring are concerned, his brother had set great store by his son, and would take his death hard, particularly when he learned there had been no kidnapping, and that Tod had simply schemed with the outlaws to get money from him.

It would be a difficult chore, but it was his place to tell John, who, after all, was his brother. John had chosen him to protect Tod from just such an end, albeit grudgingly, and when it came down to raw fact, he had failed. Had Tod been honest, and not in league with Fisk and the others—and had there actually been a kidnapping—it probably would have worked out differently. That would be the hardest part of all to tell John—that his son had deceived him.

Bray slept lightly that night, and long before the sun was visible in the sky above the eastern horizon, he was heading north. The sooner he got to Rocking Chair and turned Tod's body over to John, the sooner he could get back to the business of running down Fisk and his partners. They would account to him now—not only for the money taken but for the murder of the boy, and before it was done with he would have settled with them all.

He had held Tod in low regard, but in his resolve now he was subconsciously adhering to that curious double standard by which strong families live—which, in essence, declares that what one does to his kin is his business; what an outsider does is an entirely different matter and calls for retribution.

One of the hired hands spotted Matt as he turned into the yard late in the morning, and sent up a yell that brought others running. By the time Bray had reached the hitchrack in front of the main house and had drawn up beside Karla Wagner's pinto, several of the men were waiting, and John, his wheelchair manned by Linus Redfern, was out on the porch with the girl beside him. Bray had barely stopped, when Karla, leaving the platform at a run, hurried to him. Her eyes were fastened on the blanketed figure.

"Is—is that Tod?"

Matt nodded, shifted his gaze back to his brother. "Sorry about this, John—"

The elder Bray lowered his head. Frowning, Linus asked, "What the devil went wrong? What happened?"

Matt studied his brother quietly. A half-truth would hurt nobody, would spare John much. There was no need for him to know of Tod's duplicity.

"Had to shoot it out. Tod got hit."

John Bray still did not look up. Linus said, "They get away?"

"All four of them—and with the money."

Karla whirled to him. Her eyes were bright and color flamed in her cheeks. "You were supposed to look out for him—you, the man everybody said was a match for any outlaw! Instead you bring Tod home dead—and tell us the kidnappers got away with all the money. It—it doesn't make sense!"

Matt shrugged. "Did the best I could."

"I wonder about that," the girl shot back angrily. "It could be you planned it this way."

A coldness settled over the tall man. "What way?" he said softly.

"You didn't like Tod—hated him. Even said you wouldn't have anything to do with this ranch as long as he was around."

Bray touched Linus Redfern with his glance. The old puncher looked away. Evidently Linus had repeated what he'd said that night at the spring about having nothing to do with Rocking Chair as long as Tod was a part of it. And if the girl knew, so would John.

The older Bray raised his head. He motioned to the hired hands standing at the end of the porch. "Take the boy, put him on the bed in his room," he said, and as they stepped forward to do his bidding, he settled cold, suspicious eyes on Matt.

"You know them kidnappers?"

"I do. Man name of Fisk is one. Others are Jake Cooney, Dave Agate, and a young one they called Pete."

"I see. . . . What the girl said set me to thinking and I'm wondering myself if maybe they aren't friends of yours and—"

The anger in Matt Bray soared. "And that I was a partner with them—that what you're meaning to say?"

"Knowing what you've been in the past and the company you keep—"

"You're a damn fool, John!" Matt snapped disgustedly. "I'll tell you flat out—I never shot Tod or was in any way hooked up with—"

"Not saying it was you that pulled the trigger, even though I been told you said you would use a gun on my boy if ever it become necessary."

Linus had repeated it all—everything. Matt glanced again at the old man. He'd said nothing that night before he'd ridden out that he wouldn't have told John to his face—and he wished that he had, but it was too late now. Redfern met his eyes straight on, shrugged faintly.

"John asked me if I'd talked to you about coming back, taking over your share. Told him what you said."

"It appears to me that you're ready to come back, all right," Karla Wagner observed after a brief hush. "Only you're out to get it all, and with Tod dead and Mr. Bray all crippled up to where he can't do anything, you've fixed it so's nobody can stand in your way."

One of the remaining cowhands standing at the end of the porch muttered under his breath. Matt gave him a flat glance, turned back to his brother.

"You figure I'd do a thing like that?"

John stirred uncomfortably, brushed at the sweat standing out on his sallow face. "I ain't for sure what I think—just mighty funny to me how this here thing worked out. You feeling like you did about my boy—and then toting him home dead when you was supposed to be looking out for him—and them outlaw friends of yours getting away with all the money, I ain't—"

"Never said they were friends of mine," Matt interrupted. "Only said I knew them—three of them. One called Pete's a stranger to me."

"All that there ransom money'd be enough to make good friends over," the youngest-looking of the hired hands at the end of the porch commented dryly.

Again Matt threw a glance at the group. Linus had said the crew knew nothing about the kidnapping—or what was supposed to be a kidnapping. Evidently they had been told after he rode out.

The sudden impulse to come out with the true story of what had happened that day in the Prairie Rose pushed through Matt Bray—the need to tell it straight, give John the facts as to what had taken place—the meeting with Tod and the outlaws, his useless efforts to talk Tod out of what he was doing, his pointless ride to Sundown and back, and then finding Tod dead alongside the trail when he rode south in pursuit.

He brushed the urge aside. In their minds they had him pegged—and they were going to believe what they wanted to. The truth now would likely just make matters worse, sound to them as if he were struggling to come up with a better reason for failure. He reckoned he'd been better off if he hadn't taken it in mind to spare John, had related the incident as it had actually occurred.

"The hell with it," he said abruptly, harshly. "I told you how it was but you've cooked up something else in your head and you're dead set on thinking that's the way it was. You're wrong about it, John, but I remember you from the old days. You're too bull-headed to see anything any way but yours."

"I'm believing what makes sense," the elder Bray said woodenly. "I should've never listened to Redfern and sent for you. A bad apple's never anything but a bad apple and it don't do nothing but get rottener."

Matt shifted on the saddle, smiled tightly. "Like I said, you ain't changed," he observed, and started to wheel the bay around.

"Where the hell you think you're going?" John shouted, voice rising sharply. "I ain't done with you yet. I've a mind to hold you for the law!"

"Be the wrong move for you to make," Matt warned quietly.

"Expect he's going to meet his friends, claim his share of the money, if he doesn't already have it," Karla said icily, returning to the porch. "Then what do you plan to do—come back and take over the ranch?"

"I'll bet he's got the money right there in his saddlebags," the young cowhand at the end of the landing said, "and I'm figuring we ought to have us a look-see."

Two men near the youngster took a step forward as if to back whatever play he had in mind. Matt studied them coldly.

"Don't start something you can't in no way finish," he said, a half-smile on his lips.

"Now, you drop whatever you're thinking to do, Ferlin!" Redfern added hastily. "There ain't no sense in none of you getting yourself killed!"

"That'd not stop me if I were a man!" Karla declared, suddenly giving way to tears—of anger or grief, Matt couldn't be sure which.

"Probably a good thing you're not," he said, pulling away from the hitchrack. "You're right about one thing, however—I'll be back."

"No!" John Bray shouted. "You ever set one foot on my ranch again, I'll kill you!"

16

* * *

Forget it—let it end here!

That bitter thought filled Matt Bray's mind as he rode through the gate and headed down into the valley. John—and his old friend Linus Redfern—had made up their minds about him, based on the past and the turn of events in the present, and there was nothing he could say to change their thinking.

He reckoned he shouldn't have said what he did about Tod to Linus that night, but he'd always believed in speaking up, making it clear where he stood. He supposed he couldn't blame them for feeling as they did; he had said that the time could come when he'd be forced to shoot it out with Tod, and he'd meant it. But it would have never happened, and for one reason: Under no circumstances would he ever team up with the boy in anything, thus the situation could not arise.

But there was no use trying to explain that to his brother or to Redfern. To them he was not only capable of carrying out such a crime, but they were convinced, or nearly so, that he actually had—at least to the extent of being a party to it. And since they felt as they did, why not forget all about it, find himself a job such as he'd had when they'd summoned him, and resume the new way of life he had turned to?

Matt was finding it difficult to accept that resolution. To let Ben Fisk, Cooney, Dave Agate, and the smart-mouthed little gunslinger, Pete, get away with what they had done went against the grain—and took on the nature of a personal insult and grievance.

But above all there was the matter of cold-blooded murder, the killing of a boy—almost a man in years but not there yet—who in their hands was little more than a rank greenhorn. Their crime ought not to go unpunished, regardless of who he was. And there was the fact of not finishing a job he'd begun, something he'd always prided himself on doing. For his own peace of mind he ought to go ahead, track down the outlaws, recover the ransom, and settle with them for Tod's murder. It would then be necessary that he return to Rocking Chair, he realized, in order to deliver the money to his brother. Despite John's warning that he would be shot if he ever again set foot on the ranch, it had to be done; it was the only way he could prove them wrong about him, and while it ordinarily didn't matter to Matt Bray what others thought of him, in this instance it did.

He halted in Buffalo Crossing long enough to eat a good meal, lay in a supply of trail grub, and fill his canteen. Since he'd used his blanket to wrap Tod's body in, he needed a replacement, and this he purchased also, doing all his business at the Golden Eagle General Store, where the owner served him quickly and wordlessly and appeared greatly relieved when he departed.

It was around the middle of the afternoon when Matt was finished, and he could have lain over, spent the night in the settlement, getting an early start for the border that next morning. But he was restless and disturbed, found himself anxious to be on the move; thus, he rode on.

When darkness overtook him a few hours later, he made camp under a solitary cottonwood growing at the edge of a wide arroyo. After preparing a light supper, which he topped off with a tin of peaches, he settled back to enjoy a last cup of coffee. By the time it was finished and the fire had gone cold, the coyotes were yipping in the distance. Rolling up in his blanket, he fell asleep to the sound of their discordant choir.

He was up and on his way well before first light, a tall man riding steadily southward across the vast, bronze plains, grimly intent on a mission of personal satisfaction and vengeance.

He pulled up that night at the foot of the jagged-peaked Organs, and with the naked rock slopes glistening above him in the moon and starlight, spent the hours until dawn. Then, with the bay gelding fresh and rested, he climbed the steep trail to the pass and crossed over to the wide Mesilla Valley through which the Rio Grande flowed.

Las Cruces lay along its east bank, and several miles below it would be El Paso and the border, marked by the same sluggish stream. He'd halt in Cruces, have a talk with his bartender friend at the Amador, an inn where he often stayed, and find out for certain that the outlaws had passed through there on their way south. He was sure they would have made no change in their plans, but it was only wise to verify the belief.

There was a stranger behind the short counter when he entered the saloon late that morning. His towering figure as always drawing immediate attention from all present, Matt crossed the crowded room, recognizing none of the faces turned to him, and halted at the bar.

"Beer," he ordered in deference to his dry throat.

The crumpled-faced, bespectacled man behind the counter drew a mug full of the brew and placed it before him.

"Be a dime."

Bray laid the coin on the scarred surface. "Abe Villars around somewheres?"

The bartender tossed the dime into a box below and out of sight, folded his arms, and studied Matt narrowly.

"You know Abe?" he asked, raising his voice to be heard above the din.

Matt nodded, took a swallow of beer. He allowed the question to hang. If he hadn't known Villars he would hardly have asked for him.

"Abe's dead," the man said. "Got himself in between a couple of jaspers having themselves an argument, stopped a bullet. You wanting to see him for something special?"

Villars dead. . . . Bray gave that thought. He hadn't been in the Amador for almost a year, and Abe had been there, as usual, then.

"Aimed to ask him about some fellows we both knew. Was thinking they'd come through here."

"They got names? I been here ever since Abe got shot—could be I know them, too."

"Ben Fisk, for one," Matt said, taking another swallow of beer. "He'd be with Jake Cooney and Dave Agate, and a young big-mouth called Pete."

"They was here, all right," the bartender said a bit ruefully. "Damn near took the place apart a couple of nights ago." He paused, moved off to serve the needs of a customer tapping insistently

on the counter with an empty glass. Within a couple of minutes he returned.

"Sounds like they had themselves a time," Matt
observed casually, downing the last of the beer.

"Can bet on it—but I ain't complaining. They
paid up for all the damages they done before they
rode on."

"For El Paso—"

"Yeh, all 'cepting the one called Jake."

"What happened to him?"

"Took up with one of the women that hangs
around here. Roxie, she calls herself. Expect he's
with her right now if you're wanting to see him,
because she ain't here."

Bray had come to attention, but he kept his
manner and tone indifferent, offhand. If the bartender sensed trouble, he might forget all the
things he knew for the sake of business and his
own skin.

"Would sort of like to say howdy. This Roxie
got a place around close?"

The bartender pushed his spectacles back onto
the bridge of his nose, ducked his head toward a
door at the rear of the saloon.

"House, if you want to call it that. Only one
room. Sets on the back of the lot."

Bray said, "Much obliged," and moving away
from the bar, made his way to the exit at the back
of the building and let himself out into the weedy
area behind it. Shading his eyes against the sun,
he threw his glance to the far end of the lot.

A small shed, shaded by a single tree, stood
along its edge. Nearby was a lean-to, its open end
facing south. A gray horse was inside. Jake Cooney
had been riding a gray that day he'd met him at
the fork in Redbank Creek.

There was no doubt; it was Cooney. Reaching down, touching the pistol on his hip, Matt Bray strode across the lot and drew up at the door of the shack. Pulling his weapon, he raised a leg and drove in the sagging panel with a booted foot.

A scream greeted him as he plunged into the room. The shades had been drawn over the two windows in the wall, and though the room was dark, he had a glimpse of two figures on the bed, and then the flash of bare skin as a woman leaped from it, snatched up a robe of some sort, and rushed into a nearby corner. In the next instant Cooney's challenging voice came to him.

"Who the goddamn hell you think you are busting in here—"

Before he could finish, Bray had holstered his gun, was across the room. He seized the outlaw by an arm, jerked him off the rumpled bed, and swinging him about, slammed him up against the wall. The woman screamed again, the sound overriding the clatter of falling dishes, the crash of a picture dislodged and dropping to the floor.

"Now—wait!" Cooney yelled, recognition of the tall shape moving in on him coming quickly.

Bray drove a fist into Jake's belly, staggered as the woman—Roxie—her wits collected, threw herself onto his back. Off balance, Matt reeled against the bed, tripped, half fell. Cooney, sucking for breath, lunged past him, hands reaching for the belted gun lying on a small table close by.

Matt pulled himself upright, struggling to free himself of the woman clinging to him like a leech. Her legs were wrapped around his middle, and she was beating him about the head and neck with her fists. He twisted, caught her by an arm, jerked her free. She clawed at his face and he slapped her hard, knocked her full-length onto the bed, then wheeled hurriedly to face Cooney, who was frantically trying to get his pistol clear of the belt and holster.

The weapon came out as Matt closed in. Jake brought it up, fired hastily, filling the small room with a deafening blast and a swirl of powder smoke. The bullet went wide, and Bray lashed out, sent the pistol flying from the outlaw's hand.

In the next moment he was on Cooney, had caught him by an arm and was bending it over his knee as a man might break a stick of wood.

"Want to know one thing," Bray said through rasping gasps. "Where's Fisk and the others?"

Cooney was yelling in pain. "Gone—on to the border—"

"Where?"

"Paso—Mexican side—for God's sake, man, you're busting my arm!"

"All the same to me. Where in Paso?"

Jake Cooney moaned, swore wildly. "Saloon. Place called the Perro Rojo. Supposed to meet them there. For God's sake, don't—"

Matt rocked forward, lost his grip on the outlaw as Roxie, again coming to Cooney's aid, threw herself onto his back. Bray swore, went down flat, seeing Jake roll away out of the corner of his eye, hands groping for the pistol nearby on the floor.

Lurching to one side, Matt dislodged the woman, sent her into the wall with a hard shove. Pivoting, he drew his weapon as Cooney started to fire, triggered his own. The outlaw jolted as the slug ripped into him, then fell back. He tried to get up, lift his weapon again, but he failed and slumped to the floor.

Bray straightened slowly. Through the layers of

smoke he could see Roxie leaning against a post at the head of the bed, staring at him sullenly.

"You killed him—"

"What I come here to do," Matt said bluntly, and his breathing now levelling off, crossed to the table. A new money belt, evidently just purchased by Cooney upon reaching town, lay among the tangle of clothing piled on a chair. He picked it up, hung it over a shoulder.

Roxie swore. "You're a lousy two-bit thief! You come here to rob him—"

"Money belongs to my brother," Matt said evenly. "Cooney was in on killing one of my kin to get it."

Roxie stared at him woodenly for a few moments, and then shrugging, she picked up the robe that had fallen to the floor and drew it about her naked body.

"Might've known there'd be something wrong—man like him with all that money. Too goddamn good to be true."

"It's a tough world," Bray said dryly, and moved toward the door. He paused there, looked out into the vacant, trash- and weed-littered lot. There was no one in sight. The gunshots had attracted no one. He turned then to the woman.

"Jake pay you?"

Roxie shook her head. "Was aiming to when he left, I reckon—"

Matt opened a pocket of the money belt, extracted a twenty-dollar bill and tossed it on the bed.

"Keep half, use the rest to bury him with," he said, and stepped out into the afternoon sunlight.

17

✳ ✳ ✳

There was a satisfied glow within Matt Bray as he circled the saloon to his horse. The Perro Rojo in Paso del Norte, on the Mexican side of the river—that's where he'd find Fisk, Dave Agate, and Pete. Having forced Jake Cooney to talk would save him a lot of time.

He glanced at the sun. Several hours yet until darkness—but not enough of the day left to reach the border, a good forty miles away. Best thing to do was ride as far as he could, make camp, and line out at first light. That would put him there around mid-morning, and by noon he should have the Perro Rojo located—and the outlaws along with it.

Mounting the bay, Matt rode out of the settlement, and following the river, struck southward. It was a pleasant ride, one that took him along the grassy banks of the wide but shallow stream, sheltered almost continually by huge, spreading cottonwood trees in which doves gathered in profusion.

Avoiding the small villages and solitary farms along the way, he eventually halted for the night in a grove a short distance off the trail. By that hour the woman, Roxie, would have reported the death of Jake Cooney, and according to the account she gave, it would be accepted either as a

shoot-out—which would evoke no repercussions—
or as a murder. If the latter proved to be the case,
he could expect to have lawmen looking for him.

There was no way of knowing what she had
said, and taking no chances, he took pains not to
let himself be seen. After he had settled with Fisk
and the other two outlaws, he'd be willing to talk
the matter over with the sheriff or marshal,
whichever it was that wore the badge in Cruces,
but until then he had business to attend to.

But like as not, by that time the incident would
be forgotten, having been set down in the records
as an argument between outlaws, since no doubt
there were wanted posters on Jake floating about
the country, and the law would consider it good
riddance of another unsavory character by someone unknown—and not worth the trouble of further investigation.

Bray was up and on the move early the next
morning. He saw no one at close range, although
he did note farmers working in the fields, and
once a squad of cavalry—from Fort Bliss, he assumed—topped out along a hill to the east of him.
He waited behind a clump of mesquite until they
had vanished into the glittering flats, and then
continued.

The smoke of El Paso and its border companion, Paso del Norte, came into sight around noon,
and he began to swing away from the river, not
wanting to arrive in the center of the settlement.
Following along the base of the Franklin Mountains—barren, bleak hills of rock, from which heat
emanated in shimmering waves—he entered the
town at its lower end and worked his way down to
the river.

There he drew up in the shade alongside one of

the innumerable saloons and dismounted. Something was wrong. Ordinarily passage back and forth between the two border settlements was unrestricted, with Americans and Mexicans crossing the Rio Grande at will. But today he could see soldiers and lawmen patrolling the El Paso banks, halting and questioning all who drew near, while on the opposite shoreline Mexico's blue-uniformed *Federales* were following a similar procedure.

Bray swore deeply. To find Fisk and the others he had to get on the other side—to Paso del Norte, and the saloon called the Perro Rojo. To do so would mean running a gauntlet of questions, the nature of which was unknown, but which could result in delay and his losing out on settling with the outlaws. He'd been in El Paso's jail before, and undoubtedly there would be someone around who would remember him. While his record was now clear, he could lose days waiting for the lawmen to verify such.

Matt took a step forward into the open as a man dressed in range clothing came from the saloon's entrance, halted, turned his attention toward the river and the activity taking place along its banks.

"What's going on down there?" Bray asked, moving up beside the cowhand.

The man jumped slightly at the unexpected voice, faced Matt. "You just ride in or something?" he wondered, studying Bray irritably.

"Yeh—"

"Was a shooting down in town. Half a dozen jaspers robbed the bank—killed four people doing it. Law's looking for them to try and cross the river, hide out in Mexico somewhere."

Matt nodded. The rider turned away. He'd not press his luck. Smart thing to do was stall around until nightfall and ford the Rio Grande under cover of darkness. A few more hours, now that he was close, would make no difference.

He started to wheel, mount the bay, and find a safer place to wait out the sun, then checked himself. A heavy cloud of dust was hanging in the sky to the east. He watched it for a time, noted that it was drifting south. It could be either a herd of cattle or a train of freight wagons heading into Mexico. At once Bray swung onto the saddle, and cutting about, rode for the yellow pall. It just could be he'd not have to wait for night to make the crossing.

It proved to be a large herd of horses. The animals had evidently been purchased in Texas by a Mexican rancher and were being driven south by a dozen or so cowhands and *vaqueros* under the loose attention of a squad of American cavalry.

Matt grinned tightly. It was an opportunity made to order for him. Pulling his bandanna up to mask the lower half of his face as a deterrent to the choking, powdery film that filled the air, he waited in the mesquite until the herd had passed. Then riding out into the enveloping alkali cloud, he took a place among the scattered drovers. No one noticed, least of all the cavalrymen, who, resenting the disagreeable duty, kept themselves considerably apart, with heads down and eyes closed.

The drive reached the river, and the horses eagerly waded out into the water, halted, and began to slake their thirst. The drovers pulled off to the sides, some twirling up cigarettes while they waited, others simply loafing in the saddle. Matt, adopting their casual attitude, hung around the fringe of the herd, avoiding contact with both the Texans and the *vaqueros*.

Finally the horses had taken their fill and the shout went up to move them on. The drovers swung into action and the herd resumed the crossing as the cavalrymen turned back, leaving them unescorted, a move which raised Matt's hope for slipping away from the drive immediately upon reaching Mexican soil and for doubling back to Paso del Norte.

That hope faded just as the first of the horses splashed out of the river and gained solid footing. A dozen Mexican cavalrymen, waiting in the shade of the tall brush, rode out to meet them. The soldiers, stringing out to form a circle around the horses, paid no special attention to the drovers. Arrangements had evidently been made earlier by the owner of the stock to have the soldiers present merely in a protective capacity in the event an attempt was made by Indians or outlaws to raid the herd.

Matt, doing his part in keeping the horses on the move, watched for a chance to pull off, but it was a good three hours later, when they were well into Mexico, before the moment came. They were passing through an arroyo along which brush grew thickly. Two of the horses near him made a sudden effort to veer away from the others. Bray spurred after them, succeeded in turning them back, and then finding himself alone and unnoticed in the heavy growth, simply remained there until the herd and its escort had passed.

He was well below Paso del Norte, on unfamiliar ground, but such posed no problem. When he was certain there was no possibility of being seen by the Mexican *Federales*, he rode out of the brush and headed north and slightly west, coming into the lower edge of the settlement a time later.

He was still in an area unknown to him. Although he had visited the town several times before, his activities had been confined to the section of Paso del Norte that lay directly across the river from El Paso, where the saloons, gambling houses, and general business establishments were to be found.

There was no need to waste time asking for the Perro Rojo saloon until he reached that part of the settlement, he realized. Accordingly, he rode on, following out the narrow alleylike streets that wound between the low, flat-roofed adobe huts and wooden shacks, all with their small garden plots green with chile, corn, melon, and other vegetables. Children and dogs were everywhere, but the adults seemed to be indoors, waiting out the hot sun.

The same was true when he finally came to the business area, although the afternoon had waned and it was somewhat cooler. There were few persons abroad, and after wandering about for a time and seeing no sign indicating the Perro Rojo's location, he stopped at a small store to make inquiry. The proprietor, a small, narrow-faced man, greeted him reservedly.

"The *Perro Rojo—cantina—donde esta?*" Matt asked in his halting Spanish.

The storekeeper looked puzzled for a moment, then bowing slightly, said, "*Esperame, por favor,*" and brushing aside a curtain hanging over an open doorway behind him, disappeared into an adjoining room.

Bray could hear him speaking rapidly to someone, and then he returned. A uniformed soldier followed him. Matt stiffened as the soldier eyed him suspiciously.

"What you want?" the soldier asked.

"The Perro Rojo saloon—*cantina.*"

"Why?"

Matt shrugged. "Business. Personal."

He would as soon have avoided a meeting with any of the Mexican officials, but this had been unavoidable and he could only make the best of it.

The soldier stared, taking in his height, the clothing he wore, the gun on his hip, all the while keeping his dark features flat and expressionless. Finally his shoulders lifted, fell.

"That way," he said, pointing down the street. "When you come to the church, it is west."

"Obliged," Bray said, and keeping his movements deliberate, turned and retraced his steps to the bay, grateful the soldier had not taken it upon himself to ask a lot of questions.

Mounting, he rode on in the fading light until he came to a small church. The soldier had said the saloon would be to the west, apparently on the street that intersected at that point. Reaching the corner, Bray cut right, saw a cluster of business buildings surrounded by more huts and shacks a hundred yards or so ahead. Set off a bit apart was a square adobe structure, the mud bricks showing through in several places where the brown plaster had fallen away. Above the door of the squat building he could make out a sign bearing the fading word CANTINA, and below it in smaller letters, PERRO ROJO.

At once Matt moved on, tension lifting slightly in him as he circled to the side of the saloon in order to avoid passing before the open doorway.

Drawing up at the hitchrack alongside several horses, he halted, came off the saddle, and stepping forward, wound the bay's reins about the crossbar.

For a long minute he stood quietly beside the horse, having his look at the saloon, fixing the back door and the windows on the side nearest him in his mind. And then, a deep coolness settling through him despite the lingering heat, he ducked under the rail and started to cross the narrow strip of sun-baked ground for the rear entrance to the structure.

Abruptly Matt Bray halted. Two men had come out onto the landing. His shoulders came forward as his hands settled at his sides. It was Dave Agate and the young gunman, Pete.

18

* * *

The outlaws stood for a time talking and glancing indifferently about. Dogs were barking somewhere in the distance, and from among the nearby huts children could be heard laughing and shouting as they played. The two men did not notice Bray. In the failing light he was partly hidden by the horses, and then shortly the pair moved off the small platform and struck out across the hardpack for the first of the shacks.

Matt stirred with satisfaction. It was best he allow the outlaws to get away from the saloon. Gunfire just outside its door would certainly bring all those inside on the run—one of them would undoubtedly be Ben Fisk. And there were the *Federales* to consider also. He could expect an unusual number of the soldiers to be patrolling the town because of the killings in El Paso, and a shooting would draw their attention immediately.

He watched Pete and Dave Agate reach the first of the houses, step into the shadows filling a narrow lane that ran between them. At once he pulled clear of the horses, and his long frame bent, entered a parallel lane with the intention of circling and intercepting the outlaws at the upper end of the street.

He guessed wrong. When he cut in, believing he would be in front of the pair, he found himself

116

still behind them. The street he had followed had angled off to the left rather than maintaining a like course.

He'd not gamble again. The lanes between the houses twisted and turned with no pattern of consistency, and he could lose the two men in the maze. Stepping out into the center of the lane, he glanced to both sides and over his shoulder. Two Mexicans, clad in customary loose-fitting white pants and shirts, sandals, and wearing wide brimmed straw hats, evidently returning from the day's work in the fields, were moving off in the opposite direction. There was no sign of soldiers. Immediately Bray put his attention on the outlaws.

"Dave . . . Pete!" he called.

Agate and the gunman halted, wheeled. Even in the half-light Matt could see shock and surprise distort their features, but no words escaped their lips.

Davd Agate was the first to react. He lunged to the side, brought up his pistol as he did. Matt drew and fired, his movements a faint blur in the dusk. The outlaw's weapon discharged as he staggered back and fell, the bullet thudding dully into the mud-brick wall of a closeby hut. Bray failed to notice. His eyes were instantly on Pete, but the gunman had spun, electing not to make his try, and was plunging off into the adjacent lane coming in at right angles.

As the echoes of the gunshots rolled along the street, Bray hurried to where Dave Agate lay and hunched beside him. Ripping open the front of the outlaw's shirt, he probed for a money belt, found it. It was identical to that he'd removed from Jake Cooney. Clutching it in one hand, pistol still in the other, he came back upright and rushed on for the alleyway into which Pete had disappeared.

He could hear shouting back in the area of the Perro Rojo, guessed the shots had aroused nearby *Federales,* but he gave it little thought at the moment; they were still a safe distance away.

Matt reached the narrow, intersecting street, pulled in close to the wall of the house standing on the corner. Likely Pete would be in the doorway of one of the huts, waiting for him to show himself. Thrusting the money belt inside his shirt, Bray crouched low, peered down the dark lane. He could not see the gunman.

With the staccato barking of disturbed dogs filling his ears, Matt straightened. The gunman was in the lane somewhere—he had to be; but he could not risk waiting for the outlaw to make the first move and reveal his position. The shouts of the *Federales* as they worked their way among the huts were coming nearer. He would somehow have to force Pete's hand.

He turned, glanced back up the street. There was another cross lane a short distance on. Without hesitation, Matt pivoted, ran to it, entered, and hoping he would come to another that paralleled the one where he'd first encountered the outlaws, hurried on. Moments later, sucking for breath, he smiled in satisfaction; there was a street, one a bit wider than the other. He veered into it, and slowing his pace to a quiet walk, continued along its darkened course, filled with the rich smells of chile, corn, and mutton being prepared for the evening meal, until he gained the lane into which Pete had fled.

Again crouching low, and hat off, Bray looked around the corner. He should be able to see the gunman now—and Pete would be keeping his eyes turned to the opposite end of the street, where he expected Bray to show himself.

Matt swore softly. There was no sign of the outlaw. Either he had gone into one of the houses standing along the way, or he hadn't stopped at all but had continued running when he ducked into the side street. In either event, hunting down the gunman now would present an insurmountable problem—there were countless places where the man could hide, and he had money with which to buy sanctuary.

Matt's thoughts came to a stop. The outlaw had stepped suddenly from a deep-set doorway on down the street, had turned, and was staring at him. But Pete's lapse lasted for but a brief instant. He spun, and running hard, gained the next corner, disappeared around it.

A tight smile drew down the corners of Matt Bray's mouth. Pete would try to sucker him now. He would run no further, but halt, set up a sort of ambush of the sort Matt had anticipated earlier. Bray nodded, paused to reload his pistol, conscious of the steady progress of the approaching *Federales*. It was the way he preferred it; he was perfectly willing to face it out with Pete, take his chances on being faster.

But it must be at once. The soldiers were much too near—one could be showing himself somewhere along the street at any moment—and he needed time to bring down the gunman, recover the share of money that he would have on him, and escape before the soldiers could close in. Then he would find Fisk and settle with him.

Weapon ready, Bray crossed the lane, walked quickly to its end, and stopped at the entrance to the one into which Pete had turned. This time the gunman would be waiting; the question was whether the outlaw, driven by that strong pride common to the breed, would be out in the open, ready and willing to match skill in a quick-draw shoot-out, or whether he would seek advantage in the shadows.

Hat off again, Bray centered his attention on the narrow alleyway. The channel-like area was dim, lit only by the last of the sun's rays reflecting from the sky and by the weak candlelight from some of the windows. The sounds of children playing were gone now, and the barking dogs had once again fallen silent, leaving only the good odor of cooking food on the warm, still air.

The outlaw was leaning up against the wall of a hut only a short distance away. Gun in hand, Matt moved into the center of the street. Pete stirred languidly, raised both arms to show he was not holding his weapon. Bray let his pistol slip back into the holster.

"Been puzzling about you, Six O'Clock," the outlaw said. "All that talk about how fast you was and how nobody never could cut you down. Figured I ought to find out if it was for true."

"Suits me," Matt said. "Best we get on with it. *Federales* are close."

"Sure surprised me some, seeing you back there," Pete continued. "Was sure I'd cashed your chips for you back in the Prairie Rose."

"You about did."

Pete, now also in the middle of the lane, legs spread, arms hanging loose at his sides, shook his head.

"Reckon Jake was right about you."

"Why?"

"Said he'd only believe you was dead when he seen them planting you in the boneyard. You get him yet?"

Bray nodded. "Up in Cruces."

"Expect it was him that told you where to find us."

"Yeh, was him. You ready?"

The gunman laughed. "For a fellow that's about to die you're sure in a hell of a hurry—"

"Not figuring on dying."

"Best you do. Big like you are, you sure make a mighty easy target."

"Not what counts. Get at it, Pete."

The outlaw shrugged. "Why not? Ain't never going to find out how fast you are standing here jawing," he said, and made a sudden move for his crossed guns.

Bray's forty-five came up and fired in a single, fluid motion. Pete's weapons blasted only a fraction of time later. Matt felt the brush of the bullets as they whipped by him, one tugging at his sleeve, the other setting up a burning sensation across his shoulder.

He hung motionless for a full breath, smoke coiling about his lank figure, while the echoes again rocked along the walls of the huts, and the dogs set up their racket once more.

And then as Pete settled slowly, wearily onto the hard soil, and the weapons fell from his nerveless hands, Matt holstered his gun and hurried forward. He didn't have much time. The *Federales* would be coming.

Reaching the outlaw, Bray pulled open the man's shirt, hopeful that he, too, would be wearing a money belt and there would be no need to spend precious moments searching him. The belt was there—again one identical to that he'd taken from Cooney. Evidently the outlaws had made their purchases from the same supplier in Las Cruces upon arriving there.

"Reckon—I found out—what I—was wanting—to know," Pete mumbled as Bray stripped the leather and canvas band from about his waist and placed it with the others inside his own shirt.

Matt, straightening, looked down at the dying outlaw dispassionately, said nothing.

"You shaded me—not much—"

"Not much," Bray agreed, throwing his glance to the far end of the street. The hammer of boot heels as the soldiers approached was a hollow beat in the hush.

"Reckon it—was—enough," Pete muttered. "See you—in hell."

Bray delayed no longer. Aware of several partly open doors and window curtains cautiously drawn back in the huts close by, he spun, dropped back to the lane along which he had come. The soldiers were on the one parallel. He'd take no chances, get as far from the area as possible. Pausing to wedge match sticks against his spur rowels to silence them, he hurried on to the street beyond the next.

There he cut right, began to double back in the direction of the Perro Rojo. The lane, as he'd discovered earlier, did not run straight, however, and when he finally came in sight of the saloon, he found himself on the main street upon which it stood, and a short distance above it.

Drawing up in the deep shadows alongside a house, he considered the fairly wide roadway. Lamps had been lit in the homes and buildings lining it, and the glow from their windows and open doorways was spilling out onto the dusty ground.

There were no *Federales* to be seen—all of them apparently were over in the area where the shooting had been heard, he reckoned—but there were several persons moving along the edge of the street, which was devoid of sidewalks. Most appeared to be going nowhere in particular, were simply strolling, enjoying the coolness after a hot day.

Bray stepped out of the darkness, fell into the leisurely moving, thinly scattered flow of traffic—ostensibly a man sauntering toward the saloon. He drew abreast it, slowed, conscious of its open doorway and that he would have to pass before it and risk being seen by Ben Fisk. He could enter, seek out the outlaw—but he was unwilling to follow that course just yet; there were too many soldiers about, and when he had it out with Ben, he wanted time.

Pulling his hat low over the right side of his head, Bray moved on. There was little else he could do to disguise himself—size alone would give him away should Ben Fisk happen to be looking—but he had no choice except to take the chance.

He crossed the doorway quickly, aware of men standing just within it, of a considerable crowd farther back in the broad room, of the noise, smoke, and the smell of whiskey.

"Well, what do you know! It's old Six O'Clock hisself!"

At the greeting Matt Bray froze. The voice had come from the saloon's entrance—one of the figures he'd noticed from a corner of his eye. He swore angrily; it was a bad break encountering someone who knew him—someone who could give his presence away to Ben Fisk. Best he stop the beginning of a reunion before it got started. Fisk might not have heard. He wheeled. It was a rider he'd worked a summer with in Wyoming—Jess Craig.

"Good to see you," Bray said, taking Craig's hand firmly and drawing him away from the doorway.

"Same here! Where you been keeping yourself? Why don't we go inside, have ourselves a couple of drinks?"

They were almost to the corner of the building. Matt released his grip on Craig, shook his head. "Nothing I'd like doing better, Jess, but I'm going to have to pass—leastwise right now. Can maybe get together later, hash over old times."

"Fine, fine," Craig said. "This here saloon be jake with you?"

"Good as any," Bray replied, and then added, "like a favor, Jess. Don't mention seeing me to anybody."

Craig frowned, rubbed at the stubble on his chin. He glanced down at the pistol on Bray's hip, smiled thinly, knowingly.

"Reckon I savvy! You're here doing a little chore for somebody."

"About what it amounts to."

"All I'm wanting to know. When you're done and ready, I'll be inside, waiting."

"I'll try to make it, but if I don't I reckon we'll meet up again somewhere—if I'm still alive and kicking."

"Goes for me, too," Craig said, and started to retreat for the saloon's doorway.

"So long," Bray responded, and rounding the corner of the building, crossed to the hitchrack.

Reaching there, he heaved a sigh of relief. He'd made it back without encountering any of the soldiers. And while it had been a close call there in the doorway of the Perro Rojo, he didn't think Ben Fisk had seen him. Also, he need have no fear insofar as Jess Craig was concerned. Cautioned, Craig would keep his mouth shut.

In that next moment the satisfaction Matt Bray was experiencing drained quickly and a tautness took over. Two *Federales* had materialized from the dark lane where he had shot it out with Dave Agate and had begun the deadly game of hide-and-seek with Pete. A grim smile pulled down his lips. This would call for some fast thinking—and talking.

Leaning against the hitchrack, Bray drew out his sack of tobacco and fold of papers, began to roll a cigarette.

19

* * *

"You—*gringo*!" the older of the soldiers, an officer of some kind, judging from the markings on his uniform, said as he drew to a stop in front of Matt. "How long you here?"

Bray thumb-nailed a match, held the small flame to the cigarette he had completed, and sucked it into life. He shrugged. "Ain't kept track. A while."

"You lie, *pistolero*! I see you come from the corner," the second soldier declared angrily.

Again Matt's shoulders stirred. "Yeh, maybe I was standing there for a bit."

The soldiers eyed him narrowly. Inside the Perro Rojo a woman with a high, quavering voice was singing to the twanging accompaniment of a guitar, and off in the direction of where he'd had the showdown with Pete there was shouting.

"You are a *Tejano*?"

"Nope. Come from up New Mexico way—and on north."

The younger soldier spoke rapidly to his superior. The words were fast and slurred, and Matt, only slightly familiar with the Spanish language, failed to catch the meaning of anything said.

The officer's reply was laconic. *"Quien sabe,"* he said, and settled his dark eyes on Matt. "There was a *pistolero* such as yourself who has come here. He has slain two of your countrymen for a reason we do not know. It is believed he passed this way. Did you not see him?"

Bray shook his head. "Been several go by. Could have been one of them. You know what he looked like?"

"We are not certain," the officer replied, fumbling a bit with his precise English. "Tall, like yourself, it was said, but perhaps not so tall. We have those who were given a look at him. They will identify this killer when he is discovered."

Again the younger soldier rattled off a string of unintelligible words. The officer smiled. "My sergeant believes you are a *mentiroso*. Do you know the meaning of such, *pistolero?*"

"Nope, sure don't—and what's got you thinking I'm a gunslinger? I'm just down here looking around—and about every man I see's wearing iron."

The officer considered Matt silently. The pale yellow light from a nearby window of the saloon glinted softly on the gold braid of his uniform.

"My sergeant is perhaps correct in believing you are a liar. Also, you are a gunfighter. I am not one to be fooled. I know your kind from very long experience."

"Well, I reckon you've got the right to believe what you want," Matt said casually, glancing off down the shadowy street.

But worry was beginning to tag him. He was wishing the soldiers would be satisfied and move on. Someone might come along who had witnessed the shootings—from the cracks of narrowly opened doors and windows in which curtains had been cautiously pulled aside—and name him as the party involved.

"When do you depart Paso del Norte?" the officer asked bluntly.

Bray took a final puff on his cigarette, flipped it into the street. A small shower of sparks arose when it struck.

"Was aiming to ride out in the morning—"

The soldier shook his head. "No, it will be this night—there are too many of you here and I do not trust your words. You will be gone when I come again, *pistolero*, a time later, and if you are not I shall have you put in the jail. Is it understood?"

"Sure, whatever you say, Lieutenant."

The officer drew up stiffly. "I am a colonel—Colonel Esteban Montoya. With me is Sergeant Valdez. You will remember such."

"Whatever you say, Colonel," Matt repeated with a slow smile. "*Adios.*"

Montoya frowned, seemed on the verge of saying more, and then abruptly spun on a heel and started toward the huts, Valdez at his side. Bray, again feeling relief flowing through him, watched the pair briefly as they moved off.

They were returning to where the shootings had occurred, he knew, and he should get as far from the area as possible, but doing so was not in his mind. He still had Ben Fisk, the most dangerous of the four outlaws he'd tracked down, to settle with, and he reckoned he'd best get at it and be on his way—assuming he survived the encounter—as he had no desire to spend any time in a Mexican jail.

Both Dave Agate and Pete had been in the Perro Rojo, where Jake Cooney had said they'd agreed to meet. It was logical to think Fisk would be in there now also, as yet unaware of the deaths of his three partners.

The woman in the saloon had finished her song and the guitar had fallen silent. More importantly, the brisk click of Montoya's and Valdez' boot heels had slowed. It could only mean they were looking back from the depths of the dark street, watching to see if the officer's order to leave was being obeyed. It would be smart to ease their minds.

Casually, with the same studied indifference he'd displayed earlier, Matt drew away from the hitchrack, circled the horses standing at the crossbar, and halted beside his own. Jerking the lines free, he swung up onto the saddle. He remained motionless for a long breath, giving the two soldiers a good look at his high, silhouetted shape, and then cut back to the main street.

The squat bulk of the first building on the corner at once blocked him from view of the *Federales*. Immediately he veered right, entered a narrow lane lined with houses and small huts, his glance sweeping back and forth as he sought a suitable and safe place to hide the bay while he had it out with Fisk. Starshine, combined with lamplight filtering through the thin curtains of a window in one of the structures, revealed an enclosed yard at the rear of which was a shed. Partly concealed by the house itself, the shed was just what he was looking for.

Dismounting at once, Matt led the horse quietly through the gate into the barren yard, circled the flat-roofed residence, and drew up at the smaller building. Like most sheds, it had but three sides and a roof, but it was large enough for the gelding. Moving into it, Bray tied the bay to a rusting iron ring affixed to the wall above a trough that had once served as a feedbox.

The bay immediately lowered his head, eagerly began to snuff for grain. Casting about, Matt found a clump of thin, water-starved grass just outside the shed, and tearing free a handful, dropped it into the manger. It was poor fare for a hungry horse, he knew, but he would take care of the animal's needs later.

Standing in the shadows, he took his bearings. From the shed to the Perro Rojo would be fifty yards, a bit more possibly. He could get to the bay fast if it became necessary. The river, with Texas on its opposite bank, was to his left—north. Just how far, he had no idea, but it was of minor importance; what counted was having his horse close by—and out of sight.

Details fixed in his mind, Matt Bray retraced his way across the yard, gained the street, and returned to the corner facing the Perro Rojo, after first making certain Montoya and Valdez had not doubled back to check on his departure. Since there was no indication of them, he assumed they were still over among the huts where the shootings had taken place, where, with other soldiers, they would be searching for witnesses.

There were fewer persons abroad now, the driving heat having broken and night's coolness now taking over, making the indoors more endurable. But there were some, and waiting until an elderly man and a small boy approached from the south and started across the street, Matt fell in beside them, murmuring the customary *"Buenas tardes."*

The old man responded in kind, nodding politely, and the youngster smiled shyly. When they gained the opposite corner, and the solid, blocky structure that housed the saloon, Bray dropped back, allowed them to continue on their way, and then moved up to where he was at the edge of the doorway leading into the building.

The guitar was being strummed energetically, this time without the woman singer. Bray stood for a long minute listening to it and to the low rumble of voices, broken occasionally by laughter. Then, hand riding the butt of the pistol on his hip, he lowered his head and stepped quickly through the entrance. Immediately moving to one side, he took up a stand against the wall.

Few had noted his arrival, he saw. The bartender, a squat, dark-faced man with a thick, black mustache, watched him from behind his counter with narrow suspicion, and two of the several women available considered him with interest.

He shook his head at them, let his attention trail off and cover the dimly lit, haze-filled room. There were about a dozen patrons, some lounging about tables, others leaning against the foot-thick posts that served to support the roof. Most present were Mexicans—and Ben Fisk was not among them, he saw, unless he was behind a door in the rear of the establishment that probably opened into a private room.

The bartender, worry appeased, had turned his attention to a customer coming up to the lower end of the short bar. Matt pulled away from his place near the saloon's entrance and took a place at the counter. The bartender favored him briefly with a cold stare, moved up to serve him.

"*Que quieres?*"

"*Tequila.*"

The Mexican reached for a bottle of the water-clear liquor, poured a quantity into a smudged glass, and shoved it along with a saucer of salt toward Matt.

"*Diez centavos—*"

Bray dropped the coin onto the counter, jerked a thumb at the closed door in the back of the room.

"Card game—poker?"

The bartender frowned, nodded.

"*Americanos?*" Matt asked then, tossing off the fiery drink after placing a bit of salt on the back of his hand and touching it with his tongue.

"*Si—Norte Americanos.*"

Bray smiled, and drawing away from the bar, started across the room. He saw Craig sitting at a table against the wall at that moment. The man raised a hand, beckoned. Matt shook his head, continued to work his way through the scatter of patrons. Craig, understanding, settled back.

He reached the door, laid a hand on the knob. If Fisk was not behind it he would be faced with waiting out the man's appearance—and that could prove dangerous. Montoya, not fully satisfied that he had nothing to do with the deaths of Pete and Agate, would check to see if his orders to move on had been observed.

But one thing at a time. He'd climb no mountains until he reached them. . . . Bray gave the knob a turn. The panel, devoid of paint and bearing many scars, swung in, admitting him to a small, heat-filled room stuffy with the smells of sweat and smoke despite an open window in its back wall.

A circular table was in its center. Around it were seated a half-dozen men, money before them as they engaged in high-stakes poker under the avid attention of three or four onlookers.

Matt softly closed the door behind him, cool satisfaction again running through him. The player directly across from him was Ben Fisk.

20

* * *

Fisk was studying the cards held in his hand, a money belt matching the three others Matt had collected hanging over his shoulder. From the size of the pile of money before him on the table, it appeared he was a big winner.

"Ben—" Matt said quietly.

The outlaw glanced up, only his eyes moving. In the next fragment of time he had reacted, had lunged to his feet, gun in hand. Bray drew and fired, the shocking blast of his forty-five blending with that of Fisk's weapon. He flinched as the outlaw's bullet seared a path along his ribs, but he did not lower his gun. Instead, he held it firm and ready for a second shot. There was no need. Ben Fisk, had slammed back against the wall from the impact of the slug driving into his chest. Eyes glazing, he was sinking to the floor.

The room was in turmoil, confusion. Two of the other players were upright, were backing toward the door. Matt could hear shouts coming from the saloon, knew that shortly not only the curious but soldiers as well would be crowding in.

Moving fast, Bray circled the table, leaned over Fisk and snatched up his money belt and stuffed it inside his shirt. The open window offered a quick exit. He turned to it, came back around, hearing someone closing in on him.

"Goddamn thief—" a voice shouted.

Matt jerked aside as the speaker, one of the card players, struck out at him through the coils of powder smoke. He took the blow on the shoulder, backhanded the man with his pistol. The player reeled away, blood streaming from a cut in his cheek.

Bray felt a sharp pain in his arm, pivoted. A man, knife flashing in his hand, slashed at him a second time. Matt fired. The dark-faced assailant staggered against a chair, began to slide off slowly.

"Back off—all of you!" Matt snarled, retreating to the window.

The men in the room hesitated, glared at him. The door leading in from the saloon had opened slightly. Bray drove a bullet into the frame near the knob. The panel slammed shut instantly.

"Got no quarrel with any of you," Bray said, thrusting a leg through the window and starting to climb out. "Was with Fisk—there on the floor. Stay put and you won't get hurt."

He felt solid ground beneath his foot, ducked low, and was quickly outside. Crouched, he heard the shouts coming now from the room as the gamblers opened the door, the pound of heels in the street in front of the saloon. He looked about. He had to get to his horse fast, but it was necessary to do it with care and not allow himself to be seen.

Turning, he ran to the nearest of the huts. It was in the opposite direction from the shed where he'd left the bay, but it would be wise to circle, take an indirect route.

He reached the first of the low-roofed houses, hurried into the darkness of a lane. He became aware then of pain in his arm, slowed to examine the wound. In the pale starlight he could see that it was a deep slash just below his elbow, that it was bleeding profusely. Muttering a curse at his ill luck, he pulled off his bandanna, wrapped it about the injury, and hurried on. The burning graze left by Ben Fisk's bullet along his side was of no consequence.

The thud of men running reached him—the sound coming from behind him, and close. *Federales*, no doubt. They would have heard the sound of the gunshots through the open window—could possibly have been in front of the Perro Rojo at the time. He strained to see ahead. There were only houses standing almost wall to wall for a long hundred yards.

He turned to the nearest door, grasped the latch. It was set—locked. The pound of boots was almost on him. Bray rushed to the next hut, clamped down on the thumb trip. The panel gave. He plunged into a small room, dimly lit by candles and scantily furnished.

"*Quien es?*"

The questioning voice came from an adjoining room. Matt moved swiftly toward it, seeking the rear exit of the house. A young Mexican appeared, drew back in alarm at sight of the towering, bloodied man.

"Friend—*amigo*," Matt said, and pointed to a door in the opposite wall of what was evidently the kitchen.

He crossed to it as a child somewhere in the house began to cry, and jerked it open. The star-filled night greeted him. He sucked in a breath of relief, stepped out, and pulling the door closed, began to run along a path between stalks of corn. Instantly a dog, growling savagely, lunged at him from the depths of the garden. He struck out with

a balled fist, felt pain as his knuckles connected
with the brute's teeth, and rushed on.

A makeshift fence of tree limbs and brush
marked the rear of the property. Bray stepped
over the barrier, found himself in an alleyway. He
halted, frowning, tried to get his bearings. He
could no longer hear the soldiers, guessed they
had continued along the lane on the far side of
the house.

The shed where he'd left the gelding would be
somewhere in front of him—to the south, he rea-
soned. He had come out of the saloon, veered
north and then west. When he emerged from the
hut into which he'd ducked to escape the *Federales*, he was facing south. He needed only to continue working his way in that direction, bearing to
his left in order to stay in the general area of the
Perro Rojo.

Bray hurried on at once, following out the alleyway that suited his requirements. Shortly he
again began to hear shouting. He was drawing
near the saloon. The yells were probably from the
soldiers, making a step-by-step search along the
street.

He halted, reconsidered. He'd best keep to his
right, avoid getting close to the Perro Rojo where
there evidently was considerable activity.

"Aqui! Aqui!"

Matt Bray whirled. A soldier had come up from
behind him, was calling to the others. Instantly
Matt rushed to the side, where deep shadows
along a wall offered protection. A rifle blasted,
starting a rolling chain of echoes along the houses
and setting the dogs to frantic barking once again.
He didn't know where the bullet struck—nowhere
near him, for certain—guessed the soldier had

fired blind. But the report would serve to bring other soldiers and volunteers on the run.

He moved on, striving to make as little noise as possible, but the ground was rock-hard and his boot heels, despite all efforts, drummed hollowly. He could hear the *Federales* now in full pursuit behind him—a half-dozen or so, judging from the sound. But he was drawing near to where he'd left his horse. If he could reach there ahead of the soldiers, and not be seen as he ducked into the fenced yard, his chances of eluding them would be good.

An alleyway leading off to the left loomed before him. Unhesitatingly Matt turned into it— slowed as his eyes picked out familiar structures. He was nearer than he expected to the shed where the gelding was tethered. He had to get the *Federales* off his heels.

Crouched, he looked about for something to throw—a rock, a stick, anything that would create a sound and draw off the oncoming soldiers, make them think he had continued straight on.

There was nothing available. The lane was as clean as if it had been swept. Grim, Bray thumbed a handful of cartridges from the loops of his gunbelt. Conscious of the nearness of the soldiers, he stalled nevertheless until they were definite, dark shapes in the night, and then tossed the bullets a short distance ahead of them. He was careful not to throw them too far lest the noise they made go unnoticed.

"Este via! Andale!"

Matt, not waiting to see if the ruse worked, heard the shout, the rise of sounds as the running men reached the intersection, the gradual fading as they raced by. The scheme had succeeded. The cartridges had made sufficient noise to draw off the soldiers. Matt slackened his brisk pace, took stock of his position.

The Perro Rojo should be to his left, and yet a distance ahead. That would place the shed where he'd stabled the bay to his right—and nearby. But in the maze of similar structures it was difficult to be certain just which one it was. By day all looked much alike, in the weak starlight distinguishing one from another was even more difficult.

He moved on through the shadows. The soldiers would not be fooled for long, and there could be others in the vicinity. Abruptly he came to the end of the lane, heaved a sigh. The saloon was where he'd expected it to be. He could see its lighted windows, the horses at the hitchrack. Several men were standing about in the lot behind it, but he could not tell at that distance whether they were soldiers or merely onlookers discussing the night's excitement.

Cautious, moving slowly, Bray rounded the shack at the corner opposite the saloon, crossed its width, and turned into the lane that would take him to the house with the fenced yard, clearly visible to him now. At that moment a yell went up. Matt cursed. After all the care he'd exercised, he'd been seen, and as a sudden beat of heels reached his ears, he broke into a hard run.

He gained the yard, rushed through the gate, throwing a glance over his shoulder as he entered. His pursuers were but a short distance away and coming up fast. He'd never make it to the shed where the bay was waiting without being seen.

Light was showing faintly through a curtained window in the house. He veered around to the front of the structure, halted at the door, tried the latch. It gave. He stepped inside hurriedly, closed the panel behind him.

A woman appeared in the arched entrance to an adjoining room. Tall, dusky-skinned, and prepared for bed, she looked at him from large dark eyes that held no fear, only question as she considered him gravely.

"The *Federales*," Bray said, breathing deep, hoping that she, as was the case with the majority of Mexican people, had no use for the soldiers. "After me—can I hide—"

The woman nodded, pointed into the room behind her. "*La cama*," she said, hurriedly tousling her hair, and then as if realizing he probably did not understand the language, added, "the bed. Get in. I will come."

Matt crossed what apparently served as a parlor in two long strides and entered the adjoining, dimly lit area. Outside he could hear shouting, the thud of boots in the street—in the yard. Throwing his hat into a corner and jerking off his boots, he crawled into the bed, drew the blanket over his lank body as a pounding on the door echoed through the house.

There were a few moments of silence. The knocking, more insistent, came again. He heard the panel swing back and the woman's questioning voice. A reply came in a loud, rapid flow of Spanish. Footsteps sounded and someone halted in the archway. Bray stirred but kept his face turned to the wall.

Again there was the sound of footsteps, followed by more Spanish and the closing of the door. Voices in the yard lowered, faded. Matt sat up, started to rise.

"No, do not do so," the woman cautioned from

the archway. "The soldiers have gone but they are not to be trusted. They will come back, perhaps."

Bray shook his head. "Got my horse in your shed. Best I get out of here before they find him. Don't want to cause you any trouble, lady."

"There will be no trouble," the woman said. "And my name is Sarita."

She stepped up to the table, reached for the lamp sitting on it. "I have told them no one came here, but that I have a—a visitor who has been with me since dark," she said, turning down the wick. "If there is no light they will perhaps believe my words. But we will put no faith in such. Since they may return, I will lie with you until it is safe."

21

✳ ✳ ✳

Sarita had scarcely lain down beside him when the door burst open with a splintering of wood. A match flared and a lamp came to life in the front room, after which there was again the thump of boots. Matt raised himself partly but kept the lower half of his face concealed by the blanket. The woman had come to a sitting position beside him.

Three soldiers, one an officer holding the lamp, were standing in the entrance to the bedroom. The officer spoke in a harsh voice.

"No mi que!" Sarita replied sharply.

Anger showed on the soldier's dark face as he studied the woman. *"Puta!"* he spat out abruptly, and then adding, *"Esta bien,"* to the soldiers with him, turned back into the adjoining room. Shortly the lamp was extinguished and a scraping sound came as the shattered door was pulled shut.

Sarita waited another five minutes and then got to her feet. "It is safe now," she said, pulling on a light robe. "First I will fix the door with something so that it will remain closed, then I shall care for your wounds."

In the faint light filtering through the curtains from outside, Matt saw her glide off into the parlor, heard her drag a chair up against the panel as a substitute for its damaged latch, and then the

142

glow of a lamp once more spread through the small house as she returned.

"*Vamalos a la cocina,*" Sarita said as Matt rose slowly. At the frown on his bearded face, she smiled apologetically. "I am sorry. It is a long time since I have talked in English. Let us go to the kitchen. There I can see to the wounded parts of you."

Matt nodded, and after drawing on his boots, followed her into a third room at the rear of the house, one in which there were a table, two chairs, a corner fireplace where cooking was done, and wall shelves upon which there were numerous boxes, cans, and bottles. She motioned him into one of the chairs.

"You sure this won't be getting you in trouble with the *Federales?*" he asked.

Sarita set a bottle filled with dark liquid on the table, took a strip of cloth obtained from one of the boxes, and began to rip it into proper widths for bandages.

"It will mean nothing," she said. "You will please remove the shirt."

Bray, first taking the money belts from inside the stained, ripped garment and placing them on the table, shed his shirt, dropped it on the floor. Noting the slight wound in his side, Sarita shook her head.

"You have many injuries—"

He grinned as she started to work on the cut on his forearm, cleaning away the dried blood and dabbing some of the dark liquid into it.

"Been a long day," he said. Then, "Heard that officer say something about a *gringo*. Reckon he was talking about me. What did he say?"

"It was nothing."

"Expect it was—and I'd like to hear it."

Sarita paused, looked at him thoughtfully, her large, doelike eyes serious. In the lamplight her skin took on a mellow radiance, and her hair, hanging free about her shoulders, was jet black. Somehow she reminded him of Marcie Garrison— so calm, so quietly efficient. He frowned wonderingly; always before he had compared other women he met to Lilah.

"The lieutenant asked me why I degrade myself with an American."

"Sort of figured it was something like that. Sounded like you gave him a short answer."

The woman shrugged, resumed dabbing at the wound. "In your language what I said meant there is no difference. This cut was given you in a quarrel? Is it why the soldiers seek you?"

Matt hesitated briefly. There was no reason why she should not know. "I killed a man over in the Perro Rojo—an American like myself."

"It was for cause?" she asked, showing no reaction.

"He and three others—Americans—murdered one of my relatives and stole a lot of money. I tracked them down. Others are dead now, too."

"Here—Paso del Norte?"

"One I found in Cruces—that's a town up in New Mexico. The three others, yes."

Sarita had satisfied herself that the knife cut was clean and sterilized, turned her attention to the bandage around his head, and removed it. Apparently deciding the wound needed no further care, and that the seared places on his shoulder and along his ribs were of no consequence, she applied a fresh cloth to the head wound and returned to the slash in his arm.

Shaping a small pad of the cotton fabric, Sarita soaked it with a clear solution taken from a second bottle, placed it directly on the wound, and quickly bound it securely.

Bray, recoiling as if touched by a hot branding iron, swore softly. Beads of sweat appeared on his face. "Damned medicine hurts worse'n getting cut," he said.

"It is always so," Sarita agreed, removing the bottles and remaining bits of cloth. "You perhaps have not eaten. I will prepare a meal."

"Don't go to any bother," Bray said, picking up his shirt. "Hiding me from the *Federales* and doing all this doctoring is plenty."

She shrugged, moved to the fireplace. "It is cooked—beans with chile, torillas. I need but to warm them. There is tequilla—left here by a friend. I do not drink it but you are welcome."

Matt nodded. "Could stand a jolt, all right."

Sarita, stirring the fire into life, looked at him, puzzled, not understanding the expression. He grinned, pulled on his shirt.

"I mean I could sure use a drink," he amended.

She smiled, and crossing to a shelf, took down a half-filled bottle of the liquor, obtained a glass, and set them before him. As the woman resumed her chores at the fireplace, he poured himself a generous quantity, downed a swallow, quickly took another. At once it seemed his pulses quickened and he felt new strength stirring through his body.

"Sure what I needed," he said, and rising, went into the front room. Drawing up close to the window, he carefully surveyed the yard and the street. He could see no indication of soldiers—but that was no guarantee they had given up on him.

Chances were better than good the lieutenant had posted a man to keep an eye on the house. Wheeling, he doubled back to the kitchen.

He'd best see to the bay. Halting at the door in the back of the room, he said, "This open out to that shed?"

Sarita, stirring the contents of the kettle suspended over the fire, nodded. Close by on a flat bit of iron was a stack of *tortillas*, also warming.

"Like to water my horse, see if I can find something for him to eat. Saw some grass—"

"There is a sack of maize in the corner," the woman said. "Also there is water in the small cask outside the door—I have no well. You are welcome to both."

Borrowing the use of a pan, Bray dipped a quart or so of grain from the sack, and stepping out into the cool, clear night, carried it to the shed, only a few strides from the house. Dumping it into the feed box, he returned to the water cask, hearing the crunch of the gelding's teeth as he went to work immediately on the grain. Using one of the wooden buckets hanging from the wall, he filled it half full of water and wedged it in the mangerlike trough where the horse could get at it easily. Then he went back into the house.

Settling again on the chair, Bray poured himself another drink. Sarita was still at the fireplace, stirring the thick, savory mixture in the kettle.

"You've always lived here in Paso del Norte?"

She did not look up, simply shook her head. "I come from Chihuahua, with my husband. He was a trader. A day two years ago the Yaquis killed him. Is it impolite to ask for your name and where it is you come from?"

"Name's Matt Bray. My home was once in a

state called Wisconsin, that's way up north in the United States, but I grew up in New Mexico. Reckon you can say that's where I'm really from. Haven't been around there much lately, though."

"Are you—as the lieutenant said—a *pistolero*?"

"Done a lot of different things. Guess you could say I've had my time with a gun, too."

"But you do not now live in that way?"

"If you're asking if I hire myself out to kill a man—no. Use my gun when I have to. . . . Where'd you learn to speak English?"

"In Chihuahua. My father was a merchant, and he sent me to convent school. A nun there had knowledge of the language."

Sarita rose, turned to the shelving, and took down a plate. Crouching again before the kettle, she filled it with the mixture of beans and chile, picked up the stack of tortillas, and set it all before him on the table. Drawing back the chair opposite him, she took her place.

"Do you leave in the morning?" she asked.

"Expect I'd better," he said, rolling one of the tortillas into a loose cone and scooping into it the thick mixture on his plate. Taking a bite he nodded approvingly. The beans were tender, flavorful, and the chile had a bite to it. "The *Federales* won't give up looking for me."

"No, it is their way. But is it not possible they will be watching this house?"

"Surprise me plenty if they don't."

"Then it is best you remain here until the night of tomorrow, hide—"

Matt shook his head. "Can't do that, Sarita. Too risky for you. Obliged, anyway."

She toyed with the edge of her robe. "Where do

you go? Farther into Mexico or back to your country?"

"Aim to ford the river, get back into Texas, and head north."

"I have wondered often what it would be like in the United States. I have heard many stories—"

"Be glad to take you with me if you want," Bray said, pausing. "Can go up the border a ways, cross over without being spotted."

Sarita's shoulders moved slightly. "There would be nothing for me there—only the same life I have here. What would be the need for change?"

"Could maybe find yourself a job of some kind."

"I know nothing of work, only of the duties of a wife."

The plate was clean. Matt sat back, took up his glass of tequilla, smiled. The hard corners of his face had softened and there was no sign of grimness in his eyes.

"Sure don't know when a meal tasted so good. Expect I was hungry and didn't know it."

She reached across the table, stayed the drink he held. "There is chocolate if you wish. I do not have coffee."

"This'll do fine," he replied, and took a swallow of the liquor.

He glanced about the room, halted his attention on the door. "Glad that shed's handy from here. I'll hold off till near first light before leaving. If the *Federales* left a soldier out there watching, he'll likely be dozing around then."

"It is only a possibility—"

"Chance I'll have to take. . . . You got a flour sack or something like that I can use?" he added, laying the money belts on the table.

Sarita got to her feet, and again going to the shelving, reached into a box and procured a small, muslin sack that had once contained salt.

"There is this," she said, handing it to him.

"Just the thing," Bray said, and opening the canvas pouches sewed to the belt, removed the folds of currency and stuffed them into the sack.

Sarita watched in silence. When he had finished, she smiled. "It is very much money."

"Ought to be around twenty-five thousand dollars. Leastways there was that much to start with. Belongs to my brother. . . . I want to pay you for the favors—"

Sarita shook her head. "It is not necessary. I have no liking for the *Federales.* . . . Should you not rest before leaving?"

"Got a few hours—reckon it would be a good idea," Matt Bray agreed, and coming to his feet, followed her into the bedroom.

He was up before first light, aroused by an inner mechanism that served him as well as a clock. Sarita still slept. Carrying his clothing into the kitchen, he dressed there. Ready to depart, he stood for a time in the archway looking down at her, wishing there was more that he might do to show his appreciation than by payment, but she had refused again his offer to take her with him across the river.

That left him with but one option, and taking a double-eagle from his pocket, he placed it in the center of the table where she would find it. Then, opening the door quietly, walked quickly through the darkness to the shed where he'd picketed the bay.

22

As he led his horse across the yard Matt saw the sentry left behind by the lieutenant to watch Sarita's house. The soldier was a short distance down the street, curled up in a doorway, sleeping soundly. Bray walked the bay quietly in the opposite direction for a time, and then mounting, rode through the lanes of silent huts until the silver shine of the Rio Grande was before him.

He waited out a half hour in the brush growing along the water's edge, listening and looking for patrols. Finally concluding there were none in the vicinity, he forded the silent stream, and unchallenged by forces on either bank, entered Texas.

He continued north, avoiding Las Cruces, and after a few days steady riding, drew up at the gate leading into Rocking Chair, fully mindful of his brother's final words.

Tension began to build in him as he studied the house, not from fear but from what would develop once his presence was noted. He wanted no serious trouble with John, but he had to go through with what he had in mind, not only in order to return the ransom money and prove that he had not lied, but also to change the thinking of his brother and that of Linus Redfern, convince them he was not as low and degraded as they believed.

There had been a time when it would not have mattered what others thought, but a change had come over him—one brought on not by his memories of Lilah but by a remembrance of someone else—of Marcie Garrison and the vision of a future with her.

He realized within moments that he had been seen. Shouts went up, and shortly two hired hands appeared, hurrying up to take a stand at the corner of the ranchhouse. John, his chair wheeled by Karla Wagner, came out onto the porch. They were joined almost immediately by Redfern, bearing a rifle in his hands.

Matt grinned tightly as he viewed his welcome, shrugged as he watched his old friend pass the weapon to John. Linus was shaking his head and doing considerable talking. If Linus was endeavoring to dissuade the elder Bray from whatever he had in mind, he failed, for John levered a cartridge into the chamber of the weapon and laid it, ready, across his knees.

Matt Bray's wry smile faded. As well get it over with, he thought. Raking the bay with his spurs, he rode on, approached the house slowly. He could see all were watching him intently, and the two punchers, willing to back up their boss, were standing with hands resting on the butts of their pistols.

"Close enough!"

At John's warning shout Matt drew his horse to a stop.

"Told you I'd kill you if you ever set foot on my place again! Meant it—every damn word of it!"

"Didn't come back because I much wanted to, only because I had to," Matt called. "Got something that belongs to you."

John turned his head, said something to Karla. She leaned forward, gave him an answer, and he swung his attention back to Matt.

"Don't know what you're talking about, but come on in," he said, and hefted the rifle suggestively. "If this here's some kind of a goddamn trick—"

"No trick," Matt said.

Karla Wagner seemed to have taken over Linus Redfern's job, he thought as he started the bay forward once more. Cutting in close to the hitchrack, he circled it and drew up at the edge of the porch. Staying on his horse, he reached back, opened one of the saddlebags, and obtained the salt sack, tied at the neck with a bit of rawhide string, and tossed it to John.

"Here's your money," he said. "Expect there'll be some missing. I didn't take it—bunch that did had done some spending before I caught up with them."

Karla hurriedly came from behind John, caught up the sack. Pulling the cord free, she thrust a hand into it, produced a handful of bills.

"It is the money!" she exclaimed in disbelief.

John stared at Matt, a frown on his lined face. "You saying you tracked down them kidnappers, got my money back from them?"

Bray, still in the saddle, nodded.

"You—you wasn't one of them?"

"Told you that before. Couldn't make you believe me," Matt said coldly.

"Then I reckon you didn't have nothing to do with Tod's killing!" Redfern said, his voice carrying a note of triumph.

"No, was one of them that did it. Don't know which. Makes no difference—they all paid up."

John heaved a deep sigh. "Just never could for sure think you'd shot my boy, Matt, and I'm asking you now to forget all the fool things I said. Step down, you're at home."

Matt did not stir. Redfern bobbed, smiled wider. "Sure be good having you back—"

"Can take up where we left off talking about you and me being partners again," John added.

Bray shook his head. "No, reckon not."

"Why not? I'm needing you, Matt! Somebody's got to run the place."

"You've got Linus—and you've got the girl there. Why don't you make her your partner? Could marry her. Appears to me she'd be good as any man."

John Bray glanced at Karla, staring at him from her round, unblinking eyes. "Got to admit I've been thinking about that a bit. Ain't sure she's willing—I'm old enough to be her pa."

"Doubt if that'll make a difference to her," Matt said dryly.

He was certain of it; Karla Wagner would jump at the chance to get her hands on Rocking Chair—and it would be a good idea, a solution as far as John was concerned. Being his wife, she could take the place of the son Tod never was.

"What are you aiming to do?" John asked then in a dissatisfied voice. "Just keep on drifting—and selling that damned pistol of yours?"

"No, through with that. I've seen enough killing. There's some folks over east of here needing a lawman. Nice little town. Figure to ride over, see if the job's still open."

"You—a lawman?"

Matt shrugged. "Sure. Been most everything else," he said, and started to pull away.

"Like to ask one thing," John called.

Matt halted the gelding. "Yeh?"

"My boy—Tod—he stand up with you against them outlaws like a man ought?"

The truth was cruel—and unnecessary. The lie would hurt no one, would salve a grieving man's pain. Matt Bray smiled.

"Just like you'd expect him to," he said, and touching the brim of his hat with a forefinger, rode on.

Ray Hogan is an author who has inspired a loyal following over the years since he published his first Western novel *Ex-marshal* in 1956. Hogan was born in Willow Springs, Missouri, where his father was town marshal. At five the Hogan family moved to Albuquerque where Ray Hogan still lives in the foothills of the Sandia and Manzano mountains. His father was on the Albuquerque police force and, in later years, owned the Overland Hotel. It was while listening to his father and other old-timers tell tales from the past that Ray was inspired to recast these tales in fiction. From the beginning he did exhaustive research into the history and the people of the Old West and the walls of his study are lined with various firearms, spurs, pictures, books, and memorabilia, about all of which he can talk in dramatic detail. Among his most popular works are the series of books about Shawn Starbuck, a searcher in a quest for a lost brother, who has a clear sense of right and wrong and who is willing to stand up and be counted when it is a question of fairness or justice. His other major series is about lawman John Rye whose reputation has earned him the sobriquet The Doomsday Marshal. 'I've attempted to capture the courage and bravery of those men and women that lived out West and the dangers and problems they had to overcome,' Hogan once remarked. If his lawmen protagonists seem sometimes larger than life, it is because they are men of integrity, heroes who through grit of character and common sense are able to overcome the obstacles they encounter despite often overwhelming odds. This same grit of character can also be found in Hogan's heroines and, in *The Vengeance of Fortuna West*, Hogan wrote a gripping and totally believable account of a woman who takes up the badge and tracks the men who killed her lawman husband by ambush. No less intriguing in her way is Nellie Dupray, convicted of rustling in *The Glory Trail*. Above all, what is most impressive about Hogan's Western novels is the consistent quality with which each is crafted, the compelling depth of his characters, and his ability to juxtapose the complexities of human conflict into narratives always as intensely interesting as they are emotionally involving. His latest novel is *Soldier in Buckskin*.